The Rise of the Einix

Tina D. Miller

Black Rose Writing

www.blackrosewriting.com

ISBN: 978-1-935605-38-6

PUBLISHED BY BLACK ROSE WRITING

www.blackrosewriting.com

Printed in the United States of America

The Rise of the Einix is printed in 13.5-point Perpetua

This book is dedicated to my parents: Robert and Patricia, my siblings: Melissa, Tabatha, Tanya, and Melinda, and my extraordinary friend and personal editor, Kristina Hewis. Everyone's endless encouragement and support have been utterly astounding.

ONE

Begin a Journey Into Fire

"Do you think she can see me now?" Trixie scrunched her nose and crossed her eyes. It was the face her mother told her never to make. The girl then leaned over the ligneous casket draped in flush, silk linen.

The mother, Lola Smith, rested silently amidst Trixie's every ploy to distract her.

"She cannot distinguish you from any other tangible object in this dismal temple. Coincidentally because she is dead, she will not be able to tell you to cease this behavior, but I will. Desist your frolic," Einar, Trixie's brother, commanded her every action, including this one. He continued, "You are making a mockery of yourself, and me, for that matter." After speaking, Einar spread his hand, the width covering the girl's callow countenance, as if to shield their mother from actually seeing her daughter's face.

Trixie looked through her brother's fingers that were smudged with dirt and tears, as both twins looked over the casket and viewed their dead mother, a woman of sixty some. Few truly knew Lola's real age, since it was a detail scarcely any woman shared. Lola liked to keep secrets, her twins' existence being the most prominent of those secrets.

According to several accounts, Lola Smith died in suicidal rampage at three o'clock in the morning. She crept across the shining linoleum after ravenously guzzling an entire bottle of codeine enhanced cough syrup. Lola's creep met with a slide that eventually caused her head to meet with the kitchen counter. The syrup disabled her ability to move from the floor upon which she laid. The coroner's report would eventually read: "The mishap involved an attempted overdose of cough syrup, a wet floor, the corner of the kitchen counter, and her head". Ultimately, as everyone determined, Lola bled to death, although she had been hoping to just die quietly as the cough medicine took over. It did not, but the bleeding did. Since the coroner's report could not disclose Lola's initial intentions, one could only figure that she was tired of her grueling life as a career waitress. Plus, many said that after the birth of the twins, Lola had never been quite the same. Thirty full years of confining the twins and shielding them from society must have been mentally and physically draining, for everyone involved. It was presumed that Lola had enough. As soon as she made her bed, she wanted to die in it.

Lola was found in the deadly position atop a mass of blood splatter early in the morning. Baldric's punctual local courier found the dead woman as he tried to deliver packages of virginal spring seeds. They were seeds that Lola had been intent on planting after the last frost occurred. Lola would never have the chance to plant those seeds, and those seeds would never have a chance to grow. Death invaded the household that week. And, it was a death that Lola's adult children thankfully did not discover since they were the soundest of sleepers.

Lola's actions could not be erased, and that led the twins to this moment where death also invaded the rustic church. Trixie stared at her mother while she tried to understand the demands that Einar shouted. "Frolic", "desist", "mockery", and all the rest of Einar's ridiculously worded rants confused the girl. Trixie forgot about her brother's wishes soon enough as she surveyed every inch of her mother's face. Upon proper examination, Trixie let out a long-winded, "Eewww". She caught a glimpse of the large gash that led to Lola's undoing. Matted in the fairest of concealers to blend with Lola's porcelain skin, Lola's wound looked like a tiny mountain range forming on her face. The makeup, smudged across the silhouette, did not do the unfortunate woman justice as the gouge engorged the left side of her head.

"Half of her face looks purple." Trixie was observant and concerned. She wanted Einar to listen to her frustration of her mother's facial makeover. He did not. Obviously disturbed by the lack of attention and the sight of the dead body, Trixie released her emotions. Her sullen eyes flooded with tears as she whimpered. Still not gaining approval or disapproval from Einar, Trixie grabbed her powder puff from the feminine pink handbag hanging at her side and attempted to fix the bruise-hued mark on the monstrous face. This distracted Trixie from making her own monstrous faces.

Einar interrupted the makeover and the shed of emotion. "That is sufficient. Your badgering is enough to waken the departed." After speaking, he grabbed Trixie's hand, the one that abetted the powdering, and ended what he considered to be Trixie's childish play. Attempting to distract his sister and to continuously avoid any embarrassment, Einar turned himself and his maniacal sister away from the face of death toward the mourner-laden pews. Just as the revolution was complete, Einar vehemently whispered, "Aunt Evelyn." At the sight of the aunt, his eyes rolled, and he swung Trixie and her pink purse, which swayed in opposition to the movement, back toward the coffin so that they were staring at mortality once again. "Do not, I repeat, do not attempt any intercourse with that woman. Her drivel always progresses into some sort of atonement, just to make herself feel better. She vies for a narcissistic self-satisfaction."

"Yes Einar," Trixie responded before Einar again covered her mouth with his hand. It was another attempt to avoid any attention being drawn their way, although they, the twins of the deceased mother, *were* standing in front of the casket. Trixie, masked by her male counterpart's appendages, just stood there.

She wept. This moment of grief was symbolized by a single tear and a dribble of mucus streaming from her nose. Her facial discharge dripped onto Einar's fine grip over her mouth. Einar's grasp eventually subsided. And they, connected by a life and a death, paid their respects to their dead mother.

With their backs turned, the twins did not bear witness to their Aunt Evelyn's stumble through the hollow religious building. The aunt walked forward, directly into the back of the last pew. Upon recognizing the wooden barrier and upon recognizing the situational death that led her into the church, Aunt Evelyn grabbed her long flowing black dress and maneuvered more cautiously down the aisle, one foot in front of the other as her hands clasped a shining silver flask. It seemed as though she was mimicking a bride holding tightly onto a fresh wedding bouquet. Yet, her face mimicked something more evil than a blushing bride. Her quivering, taut lips could not mask the smile that hid underneath, and her eyes were scarce of any benevolence.

Acknowledging the sound of pandemonium, Einar, with much bravado and perhaps even more pride, faced the crowd, turning Trixie with him. He awaited recognition from the aunt, yet he was also able to camouflage his presence and that of his sister from the aunt because of the aunt's unreceptive awareness. Aunt Evelyn, as she continued her walk through the dimly lit house of a god, assembled hastily in Baldric's most desperate times, looked as if she could barely remember why she was there, again. Even if not medically diagnosed, she certainly lacked a short term memory. Although at a serious affair, one that should bring family closer, Einar couldn't help but to whisper his observations of the disheveled aunt into Trixie's ear. "Look, she brought refreshments. Oh the incense of gin! Yet, I am sure, nestled in the crevices of her dress of mourn, she has anything you could ask for: bourbon, vodka, and even a miscellany of mixers." Einar turned himself and his twin away from the eyes of the observers. It was not an appropriate time for amusement.

Trixie briefly forgot about the deadly situation and laughed hysterically at her brother's cynicism of their aunt. She laughed as if she understood, but honestly, she did not comprehend any of it. Soon enough, the laughter increased, and Trixie was awkwardly doubled over her own mother's coffin. The force of her body movement tossed Einar forward also. As Einar looked into the casket, he shivered. It was the first sign of grief from the twin who disliked his mother immensely. Momentarily though, Einar's dislike of his mother was shielded by the graven image and the sound of his sister chuckling.

As the twins were both closer to death than they would have liked, Aunt Evelyn finally spotted them, her own motherless niece and nephew. With her jaundiced eyes and pallid skin, the aunt snuck up behind the siblings. The twins were so distracted by the vision that Einar so aptly described and the innate body that laid in front of them that they entirely forgot to conceal their presence. It probably wasn't possible anyway.

Aunt Evelyn approached them and spoke, "'Tis impolite to giggle over a dead woman's body, especially that of your own mother." The voice startled the duo, and it caused both twins to jump. Neither of the Smith children appreciated the screeching pseudo English accentuation of the drunken aunt. The voice persisted. "Now you two move so that I can see that darling face of your mother's one last time. Anyhow, Einar, I need you to fetch a damp rag. My emotions are troubled, and I wouldn't want anyone to have to look after me if I fainted."

Her unknown sarcasm caused Einar to look at his sibling and smirk. Trixie smiled back just because her aunt always seemed to be quite silly. Recognizing the ridiculous circumstances that Aunt Evelyn often created, Einar entertained himself with visions of taunting the imbecile (a name he often used to indirectly address the woman, his aunt). When the visuals ceased and Einar soon recognized the situation at hand, he replaced his grin with a scowl and spoke, "Yes, Miss Evelyn, I, we, will fetch you a moist cloth." Einar blatantly ignored his aunt's familiar relationship with him and his sister while attempting to remind her of her marital status. It was something that he blatantly always attempted to do.

Aunt Evelyn ignored the label meant for single women. She was too occupied fearing a lack of understanding on Einar's part. They did, after all, have different vocabularies. So, she reiterated, "A wet one."

"Yes, a wet towel. We will retrieve a wet towel for you, your highness." Einar faced the aunt after speaking. Trixie followed suit. Einar then bowed toward the aunt, and Trixie did the same. Neither was very serious. This was evident when Trixie began to snicker. She liked when Einar was silly and pretended to be a member of English royalty. Einar liked when Trixie thought all English were royals. Both entertained one another for entirely different reasons. It worked.

The twins stood upright and began to walk away from the aunt. Einar was especially elated to move beyond the personal space of the drunkard aunt. He was also relieved to swiftly escape the looming feeling of death that even the wooden church rafters could not rise above.

The twins walked from the sanctuary through the nondescript corridor into the foyer of the religious structure. The entryway was where conversations normally turned from whispers into more casual tones. This time was no different. The noise was boisterous, and the air was filled with gossip and juicy details surrounding the dead woman's life and death. But, as soon as the twins emerged from the depths of the sanctuary, the conversations quieted. This immediate response was alarming. Lola was not going to be the only topic of conversation. Although the people were shocked and pleased by the death of Lola Smith-a scandalous, infamous tramp in the town- the people were even more intrigued by the Einar and Trixie. They were a scientific spectacle that most people had never seen. Some, who had randomly spotted the twins, called them clones. Others, especially those who had never caught sight of the duo, labeled them freaks. The only medical diagnosis that the twins knew of was that they were twins. Nobody in the town of Baldric had ever lived among twins, ones like them, who functioned in society. That was entirely the faults of Lola and the twin's natural predisposition.

After entering the entryway, Einar shifted through the crowd and made way for him and his sister. The crowd parted in two. The twins crept through and interrupted the quietness with the rustle of their legs and bodies rubbing against one another. Einar, with an awkward grace, flowed along the oriental burgundy runner. Trixie followed along with him. No one spoke to them directly as they passed. The gawkers just stared; pity marked the people's faces as they concurrently mumbled to each other.

All the pitiful eyes continued to follow the innocent twins who traveled along the plush, red runner. The twins did not stop to greet the eyes watching; they just continued their efforts to find the restroom. Luckily, past the crowded mass of stalkers, a subtle light aided Einar and Trixie. They journeyed through the divine erection that the hard working members of the Baldric workforce built with their meager, less than divine, charities. The nearly stolen monies were used to create the lavish ambiance of the Bapterian church, including all of the expensive fixtures. One such fixture beheld a light that became an illumination that shone upon Einar's and Trixie's faces. The glare accentuated the pink freckles that sprinkled the noses of both twins and the vivid gray eyes, all four of which were fixated intently upon the end of the hallway and the origin of the light.

The twins had similar, almost identical features, especially their oddly shaped ears that stood out through the chin length, dirty blond hair that was also emphasized by the lighting. The

11

radiance was calming, and Trixie felt that the ray of light was a sign of divinity, or, if she could put it in her own words, "really special". Ironically, the misleading seraphic stream did not derive from one of those heavenly lights that coaxed all who laid eyes upon it to follow; it was the immaculate brilliance of the lavatory. And, it was a nice, partial deviation from the prying eyes.

After many dooming steps toward the lavatory, the stone-faced, curly haired twins finally made it into their haven and stopped, momentarily, upon hearing the clink of the latch on the door that closed behind them. They successfully escaped the drudgery that had just ensued.

"Why do I feel so dirty, so icky? Why was everyone staring?" Trixie commented. She smoothed her hair and stared into the mirror of the family restroom. She did feel soiled by the obtrusive eyes that stalked her every move and the vacant eyes of the god that apparently overlooked the church and beyond. Even Trixie's own eyes reflecting back at her could not erase the current, vivid memory of complacent mourners watching the movement of the twins who aptly marched onward past the crowded mass of stares.

Einar knew better than to explain to her that the few that they had been in contact with always looked at them that way. He did not have time to react to society's reactions of him, his twin, and the death. Instead, he was motivated to fulfill his aunt's wishes so that he could escape any wrath that always included drunken slaver that flew out of her orifices. He quickly grabbed several paper towels and ran them over the streaming warm water. As he wrung the towels to a perfect moistness, he reminded Trixie of their parental state. "Mother is in an eternal slumber." His voice wavered, sending sounds of a calm distress. It was one of the few times that Einar's emotions confused him. He was slightly hurt and saddened by the death of his mother, but he did little to show it, until now. His and his sister's world was not fitted comfortably upon his shoulders.

Trixie looked at Einar befuddled. She too was confused by the saddened tone Einar rarely ever used and unsure as to whether her mother was sleeping or dead. Unfortunately, their mother was gone, and their father was a traveling salesman, whose name had not yet been revealed to the twins or any other citizens of Baldric. The man traveled into, through, and quickly out of the town, as far as anyone knew. Lola's and the salesman's affair was brief, around ten minutes. These ten minutes did not include the previous half hour he spent schmoozing her while she was working as a waitress in the local diner, a revered eatery in the town of Baldric.

Einar didn't explain all of this to Trixie as he was more concerned with hiding the tears welling in his eyes. This momentary sadness was not because their father was seemingly nonexistent; he was. The root of the sadness was because Einar fully realized that it would be him who would shelter his sister; they would have to approach the world together. It was the first time in thirty years. No mother was there to keep them in the confines of their home. This commencement marking their own freedom was a daunting task, one that would impede on any personal endeavors that he had dreamed of accomplishing for much of those thirty years. But, Trixie was his sister, and nothing could break their strong sibling bond.

"You belong to me. I, you," Einar explained. These were details Trixie did not understand. These were details Einar wished to ignore; he couldn't.

Trixie, whose emotions remained consistently confused and somber during much of the ordeal, did not understand the gravity of their motherless situation. She, due to Einar's previous explanation of Lola's slumber, was just under the impression that her mother was sleeping for a long time, and it was time for Trixie to become the woman of the house. She figured that witnessing the process of death or a long slumber was a mere ritual into

13

adulthood. Perhaps she was right.

Her thoughts continued with the people at her mother's funeral and her dead mother. "Momma was a nice person; we are nice people. Not everybody has to look so mean." Trixie did her best impression of a mean, dirty person in the mirror that Einar was trying to avoid looking into. Something dirty always stared back.

Before Einar could even respond, the church bells interrupted the images. It continued to stun the ears of all of the churchgoers throughout the worship asylum. It was the proper noise to remind all that it was time to listen to the rhetoric that Baldric's reverend had to offer. The chimes were the perfect cue to the twins that they should make their way back to the dungeonous room that housed the dead mom, the ravenous aunt, the menacing multi-denominational reverend, and the other curious bystanders. And that they did, returning unscathed.

TWO

The Vested from the Funeral Pyre

Beginning with the day of the death through the day of the lengthy sermon until the day of the reading of the will, the twins spent more time in the realm of society than ever before. This was, along with the death of their mother that left them homeless for several days, the root of much of their anguish and emotional drainage. Reluctantly, the twins found sanctuary, yet little solace, in the confines of the church pews, offered to the folk of Baldric during the most trying of times. The twins' trying time was partly the result of the church's Ladies Mission that refused to allow them to reenter their contaminated home until all visible reminders of their mother's death were erased by a strong mixture of cleaning fluids.

In order to listen to the last will and testament of Lola Smith, the virtuous twins, from one less than virtuous institutionalized location to another, arrived at the Law Office of Kluge and Kluge. The office was situated next to the Baldric's Bapterian Church where the reverend often commented, "The aid of the church and the law shall guide you." It was simple advice for the simple people.

The large marble and glass structure that housed the law office and the ornament-adorned church stood out from the tenements and the other scattered, tattered buildings in the economically depressed town where miscellany sexual deeds often substituted for other forms of payment for necessary, tangible items. It was an economic system that could not fail.

Loki Kluge was the local attorney, faulted, like everyone else, for accepting sexual bartering. He deemed his law office would give 'more bang for the buck'. It was a clever tactic, and many, even those not in the town, sought out the skills of the overzealous lawyer. Although his business was successful, monetarily and otherwise, Kluge still disappointed his family by not following in his ancestor's footsteps and becoming a participant in Kluge's Traveling Circus. Although, when the circus traveled into the town each year, Kluge was willing to coerce the most interesting of characters he encountered throughout each year to join the assemblage. He insisted that the most bizarre peoples were the ones who sought out his lawyer skills the most. It was insightful on his part. In a time of economic depression, the law business exploded. Kluge and his family used this platform to the best of their abilities.

As a lawyer and friend of the circus, Kluge worked tediously to appease the disturbed patrons and concurrently find employment for them also. Ultimately, his acclaimed success enabled him to a more prestigious lifestyle, one that could not be broken by a myriad of his questionable tactics. One unusual policy was his attempt to apply any convictions of his clients to himself. This ended hastily as Jojo Pertro, an insurance agent, knowingly deceived many of the members of Baldric. When convicted and sentenced to Baldric's minimum-security prison for a sum of many years, Kluge backed out of the deal. He knew that jail time would impede on his personal satisfaction, any future triumphs, and his personal freedom. He ignored the sentencing for several months until he knew that the educationally disadvantaged folk would entirely forget about his promise. It worked, and Kluge was not held to his word. He was a lawyer after all, and luckily for the twins, Kluge's defense skills were not needed; he was, conditionally, just the executor of their mother's will.

Einar and Trixie followed the maze of hallway that was decorated with an assortment of relics of Kluge's success. The twins graciously stopped and scanned the man's achievements. Einar read the script on the plaques while Trixie just viewed the pictures and stared at the "shiny gold" of the wall hangings. Their adventure led the twins to a large, double door that welcomed them into a rectangular room. It was the conference room, suitable for conferences, meetings, and will recitations. It was the most appropriate place for what would ensue.

When the twins entered, they ventured toward the podium and then sat on the nearby wooden folding seats arranged in the front row. They were surrounded by the peaceful sounds of calming elevator music that could have lullabied anybody to sleep. Simultaneously, the twins crossed their ankles and settled into the comfortless, armless seating. They posed upright and awaited any news of an inheritance, although Lola did not have much to offer to the twins or any other town member. The deceased woman's material possessions were scarce and cheap, except for her massive collection of antiquated wooden measuring instruments that also served as suitable forms of weaponry and entertainment for the Smith household.

Einar and Trixie were amateur fencers, by design of their confinement. They often used the makeshift, wooden swords to practice their craft. Proving unsuccessful swordsman and woman, the twins measured the house or build small yardstick cabins within which they could hide, as if their confinement did not hide them enough. The yardsticks proved multifunctional, as Lola also used the measuring instruments in unsavory acts. These were the yardsticks by which she measured her men.

Aside from her reputable collection, Lola had always believed that material possessions did not feed the soul; sexual offerings did. Obviously her soul was not fed well enough, and finally she realized that it was not the sexual encounters that would help her find her identity. It was a poignant observation by a tramp in a town where sex spent as money. The twins knew nothing about sexual prowess or Baldric's economic system. Lola thought it better that way. And, aside from the control she held inside of her home, the only other control that Lola could grasp was death, lingering within her reach.

"The yardsticks, the pictures, the house…" Einar began to verbally list the items that could be inherited. This did not distract Trixie from the noise as she tapped her foot to the mundane and monotone melody of the music that repelled off of the sound proof walls. Trixie could have cared less with material possessions, only because she didn't know any better. Einar's ramblings and Trixie's delicate thumps were interrupted by a storm of people huffing and puffing from the tremendous jaunt up the multitude of stairs laid to mimic the most revered of Roman architecture. The twins' behaviors ceased, and the music became nearly indistinguishable from the ambient noise surrounding the twins. Almost all of the 132 spineless, witless populace, except Mr. Pertro and recluse Old Man McCormick, were encouraged to attend the public meeting, and surely enough, that is what they did. The people of Baldric left the church and other places of business empty for the afternoon. It was quite an abnormal occasion, especially because Kluge had never actually read a will aloud. Lola, though, before her death, insisted upon a live reading after her death. In fact, she even purchased, with real paper money, several boxes of the quaintest invitations. She was fully prepared to leave the life that she had been entirely unprepared to live.

The room filled, and Trixie was quite amazed at her mother's popularity. She was ignorant of her mother's sexual forays, which ultimately made her mother so "popular". Trixie sat, mouth agape, and watched the people, while Einar helped to explain some of the intentions of the curious members of the decrepit town. "There's

Mr. Dourty and trailing, Mrs. Dourty. Mother convinced the man that an affair was in order since he wore her favorite men's cologne. He admitted the same of her wanton scent and then attempted to deceive the vows of his nuptials, until it came time to do the deed. He backed down and then backed out of her car. He claims to have been scarred by the whole ordeal. Mrs. Dourty, who is certain something occurred with her husband and Mother, claims that he no longer settles his gaze upon her the same." Einar knew of Lola's scandalous adventures because, out of spite, he had read Lola's appropriately self-titled "Diary of Carnal Desires and Deeds". He read of his mother's clandestine activities while she was trolloping about the town. In fact, Einar spent most of his adult life trying to learn everything secret, to be used as blackmail when necessary, about the woman who kept him confined and unable to experience all that life had to offer. And, to keep Trixie off of his trail, he would tell her it was the *Bible*, a book that even the slightly, mentally underdeveloped twin could recognize.

Einar, of course, was unable to appropriately use the information he had obtained, so he opted to disclose some of it to his twin. It was an opportune moment. He found self-satisfaction in sharing some of the details of Lola's excursions and trysts. Trixie, unresponsive to any of the information offered to her, focused on the conversations that were more audible than Einar's whispers. She was visually curious but not quite mentally. In the midst of her mindless thoughts, Trixie pointed toward the door, leaned closer into Einar's ear, and screeched, "What is *she* doing here?"

Trixie's reference was to Madam Eleanor, Lola's neighbor. Trixie knew that the neighbor was an enemy of the family. As a child, adolescent, and young adult, Trixie would sit at the windowsill while her brother would sit next to her reading something that he called the *Bible*. Although trying to understand more simple things, like the birds singing to her, Trixie was always distracted by the screaming rants of Mme. Eleanor. The next door neighbor used enough of those bad words, the words Lola told Trixie never to utter, that Trixie knew the neighbor was no friend of theirs.

Trixie was correct in her observation. Mme. Eleanor was no friend of theirs. She was the igniter of a feud that had been going on for several months. The feud was fueled by a willow tree. And, it was assumed that Eleanor nearly stalked the woman and would have done so every day until half of Lola's tree's limp branches sweeping across her yard were disbranched or at least trimmed. "That bitch's death," she would forthright explain, "is not good enough, god damn it. She could have at least trimmed the branches before she offed herself. God damned whore." At least, that was the mme.'s opinion of the situation before she attended the reading of the will. It was probably going to be her opinion after the reading also because it was rumored that she actually saw Lola lying on the floor of the kitchen while attempting to visit the Smith homestead at the crack of dawn specifically for confrontational purposes about the willow tree branches drooping into her backyard. Trixie knew not to like that woman, so she stole her attention away from the enemy.

The reading chamber, although modest by comparison to the rest of the opulent office building was larger than most people's living rooms and had become quite full of erratic, vehement townsfolk devilishly content that Lola was dead. Before Einar could answer Trixie's first question about their neighbor, Trixie began her inquisition again. "And *her?*" Trixie continued pointing as the stampede trickled down to a few random, late entrants. Trixie's latter question actually referred to Aunt Evelyn, someone Einar expected, even though he believed that she did not deserve anything. She had certainly been a menace to the twins, and Einar suspected that it was her idea that Lola sheltered the twins. Even when the twins were younger and obviously much cuter than their adult selves, the aunt sneered at them, almost in disgust. After a while, the woman stopped visiting her own sister, causing anguish between the women. Evelyn was hopeful but unsuccessful at achieving the status of Baldric's Jezebel. And with Lola's death, Baldric was sans one frisky female vying for the gentleman's affections for nothing but pleasure. Evelyn was pleased at finally becoming the rightful heir to the title Lola once held. At least, that was what most of the men, married or not, probably hoped for.

"Can she go anywhere without being entirely annihilated?" Einar's comment, like many he made of his aunt, made Trixie giggle. The word "annihilated" did seem funny, and suddenly the feminine twin lost awareness of her intentions with the pointing and questioning.

As the twins continued to survey the crowd, which continued to survey the twins, Mr. Loki Kluge marched in. He was donned in a blue pinstriped suit with oiled, slicked back hair, the type of hair one expected on such a tall, successful man. Before Kluge addressed the crowd, he took a padded mallet and headed toward the bronzed gong in the center of the conference room. As he passed the open window, the red floral curtains waved to the crowd. Einar felt his mother's presence in the room while Trixie just felt a mere breeze. "Ooohhh, that makes me chilly."

"I feel it also," Einar retorted, although he was referring to something else.

Before Einar could further explain, Lola's words became alive in the room bedecked with greedy peasants as Kluge began the reading of the will that had been created only days before Lola's death.

"Welcome," Kluge began. "We have gathered today to interpret the will of Miss Lola Smith. Any questions?" Kluge waited for mere seconds before he spoke again. "Well, if everyone is comfortable and if everybody understands, I will begin." Kluge cleared his throat with the most distinguished of "ahems" and took a deep breath.

As Kluge prepared his vocal chords for the read, a lull loomed throughout the room until Mr. Hartfoam, a man of petite stature and quite a lack of timeliness, rose from his chair, even though it looked like he was still sitting, and squealed, "Is this will particular? Am I wasting my time being here? My gardenias need to be watered, and I could hoe my garden this lovely afternoon if I don't have to be here." The crowd muttered in agreement that his yard did actually need to be hoed and his flowers were looking a bit deathly, yet not as deathly as the recently deceased. Mr. Hartfoam was one of the few men who was not measured in Lola's proverbial little black book.

"Yes, the will is particular. Quite particular. If you are here, it is for a reason. Anything else?" Kluge questioned.

After several moments of silence, a choir of voices floated through the air, yet none were specifically audible. With a brief shush from Kluge, the noise quieted once more.

"Well then, I will begin." With that premise, Kluge swung the mallet and pounded the gong just once with much intensity. The "boing" resounded throughout the room, and the attorney waited until all was silent again. He smoothed his suiting and did the same to his oil soaked hair. When all was in place, he initiated the reading and read the script almost word for word, just as Lola had coached him to do.

"This will was assembled by a said Miss Lola Smith with assistance from a said Mr. Loki Kluge, me, several days prior to…" Kluge looked down. He was unable to finish his last statement. With as much professionalism and as little emotion as he could muster, Kluge began the next sentence, rendering the first statement a failure. "All information stated in this legal document is notarized and thus, legal. The contents of this document cannot be negotiated, as all particulars were created and looked over by the deceased." He stopped to take a breath and then continued, "Before, of course, she was deceased. May we take a moment of silence?" Kluge did not wait for an answer as he instructed, "Silence, please."

Kluge needed the moment to recall the events of the day that he last saw Lola. She sat atop his desk. She was outfitted in a provocative, red outfit. He remembered the faux silk and lace. He also clearly remembered Lola's insistence upon the living will. This confused him, so he questioned it and then questioned their relationship. Lola clearly declined to answer the questions and then reminded Kluge of their relations, not relationship.

Kluge was still standing in front of the crowd, taking more than a moment of silence when he reminisced rubbing Lola's thigh for the last time. She swatted his hand away. Kluge's ego was wounded, and he never again questioned the woman, in part because that was the last time that he had seen her. She did not even pay for his services.

After refocusing himself, Kluge spoke slowly as he began the actual translation of the will. His voice lifted to a much higher octave, as if to impersonate Lola. They were obviously her exact words printed on a legal pad. The small print of the script caused another awkward pause, as Kluge had to lean over and squint at the fine lettering.

"I, a one Miss Lola Smith, do bequeath to Big Al of Big Al's Diner all of the kitchenware, plate ware, and frozen desserts, the ones that are left, that I have taken without permission. I am not rendering myself a thief; I am just returning borrowed goods. Next, I bequeath to Mr. Elliot, my postman, Fluffy the stuffed dog, who, when alive before the birth of the twins, used to bite him on the leg and yelp a severe greeting as he approached. I bequeath to my horrendous sister Evelyn my collection of antique liquor bottles and the more current bottles as well. She is also allotted the entire contents of my liquor cabinet, including any cooking wine, in hopes that she will drink herself into oblivion and soon join the rest of the heathens in hell."

Evelyn, clearly hearing of and agreeing with her sister's wishes, brushed her fake tears, shaded with jet black mascara, away with her quivering, wrinkled hand. The thought of her sister leaving her anything other than a respectable list of clients made her appreciate the deceased. Plus, it was liquor that she was given. That made her smile beneath the tears of joy.

"I bequeath to Mr. and Mrs. Dourty, my collection of lingerie and mail order perfumes from around the w-w-world." Kluge stopped for a moment to allow his nervous stutter to cease before he continued with Lola's wishes. The sexual prowess of the lawyer who visualized Lola surrendering herself to Dourty caught Kluge off guard for the second time. The first time was when Lola was sitting in his office outlining the necessities of the will.

When Kluge's emotions eased, he continued with his high-pitched portrayal, "I hope this will reignite any passion you have had for one another. I bequeath to Madame Eleanor my gardening sheers to trim, yet not dismember, the branches of the darling willow tree. May it stand in memory of me."

Eleanor was unhappy with the demand and shared her disagreement with the room. "That whore. That tree-hugging tramp."

Kluge quickly interrupted the woman's verbal regurgitation. He continued the reading and added a lengthy list of bequeaths to a multitude of people. Even Kluge was a recipient, as Lola bequeathed her bedroom linens to the man. She was aware that Kluge would enjoy the reminiscent scent of her sheets. Lola, before her death, was quite cognizant to the needs of the people. In fact, everyone sitting in that room received something. The yardstick collection attributed to much of the length of the reading. The dead woman wanted to make damn sure that even if she was dead, good memories of her (because of her charitable donations) would live on, even if only a handful of people ever had a good thought about her.

Through Kluge's rambling, Einar caught Trixie yawning. "You must look more alive than mother on her day of eradication."

For a moment, once again, Trixie thought that perhaps her mother wasn't dead. Before she could ask what an eradication was, her attention shifted from Kluge and his seemingly long-winded and exasperating list toward Aunt Evelyn. She sat three rows behind the twins. To evade any boredom on her part, Aunt Evelyn sipped on her contained gin. The twin watched Aunt Evelyn as the metal of the flask hit the woman's sunken, cracked lips that were smothered in Avon's most alluring, signature red from 1940.

"To the twins, Einar and Trixie, my children, I bequeath my estate." Kluge's voice now switched from being the interim Lola's to his own. This tactic was suggested by Lola who figured the twins might take the message more seriously if Kluge used his own raspy voice. He spoke, "These items are contingent upon the twins both holding a job to maintain the upkeep on the house. Guardianship of the twins, although adults, will be determined by their abilities to maintain themselves and their home. If they cannot, they will become dependents of their closest relative, that being Ms. Evelyn Smith." The twins, because of their situation and mental and physical capabilities, which for the girl twin was quite limited, were not expected to be able to function on their own. That was certainly the message that Lola sent to the people of Baldric for thirty years. That was certainly the message that the people of Baldric were sending to the twins.

As Aunt Evelyn heard Kluge's words, her hands let free of the smooth metal container that had in no time fallen to the floor in an echoing clunk that became a melody to the subtle gasps of the woman. It was a harsh reality to all, especially the drunken, irresponsible aunt who wanted nothing more than to bear her own children, not take care of ones that have been conceived and birthed by others. Anyhow, the twins were adults and needed to learn how to fend for themselves, just like everyone else had to.

The crash of Evelyn's flask startled the lawyer who wanted nothing more than to end the tedious process and bury Lola deep within his memory. In hopes to flee to the confines of his office, Kluge, utilizing his own masculine sound, commenced the finale of the reading. "I, Mr. Loki Kluge, do hereby announce that all of the items in this will of the said Miss Lola Smith are final and, again, non-negotiable. If there are no questions or concerns, you may dismiss yourselves from this reading." With that, he once again banged the gong more harshly than before. He gathered the items that layered the pedestal, his stride bounding toward the door. As he rushed passed Einar and Trixie, Kluge obstructed his own forward motion. He leaned between the twins' ears, startled them for a moment, and whispered, "Twins, I need to see you. We need to discuss the technicalities of this reading. Please meet me in my office." Kluge pointed and added, "Across the hallway."

Kluge, freeing himself from the watchful eyes and devastating shrieks of the attendees, continued on as the twins arose and followed the procession of the slowly paced gift recipients behind the lawyer and headed in the direction of the real office of Mr. Kluge.

THREE

Entailing of the Intricacies

The hallway between the reading room and the law office, only moments earlier teeming with curious members of Baldric society, emptied as the twins awaited the arrival of Kluge. He was obviously finding a moment of refuge elsewhere. After experiencing the menacing stares and listening to the curious whispers, the twins' patience dwindled.

"Should we?" Trixie prompted as she pointed at the door. She didn't have to finish her statement. She was clear enough for Einar to understand. With the man of law nowhere in sight, the twins opted to enter the office instead of lingering in the hallway. With a synchronous push, they opened the large doors of patterned oak to find a small room with little décor being shielded by the intricately designed entranceway. Positioned in the center of the room was a desk which held a much more respectable stature than the man who sat behind it. Einar and Trixie found their way onto the lovely floral couch on the east side of the room.

"This is nice." Trixie liked nice things.

"What?"

"This couch. It reminds me of a dress mama used to wear around the house."

"You must be referring to her house coat."

"It wasn't a coat. It was a dress with big white buttons down the front."

"And where are the buttons down the front of this couch?"

"You know what I mean. The flowers, they remind me of… hey, who are those guys?" Trixie hoisted her attention to the two large pictures that framed the window behind the desk.

"The man on the left," Einar pointed to the one on the left in case Trixie did not understand what he meant, "is former President Abraham Lincoln. And the one on the right," Einar now moved his pointer slightly over to the right, passing the window in its path, "that is former President Thomas Jefferson. Either Kluge is thoroughly politically confused, pays homage to a diverse population of presidents, or he is sending a message about seeing both sides of any issue." Einar, brash in his assessment of Kluge, knew many steamy details about him. Einar disliked the man. He disliked the man. Plus, Einar was disheartened by the fact that Kluge was unable to admire only one of the political parties. The male twin continued his rant. "Lincoln and Jefferson were essentially foes, belonging to entirely separate parties. Can we not maintain personal, political identities via one party platform?"

"Huh?" was all Trixie could utter. She was lost from all of the pointing, let alone all of the banter that Einar just yammered into her ear.

"Never mind."

"That's nice. I wonder if mama had any pictures of presidents that we can look at. I would sure love one on my wall."

"Indeed. If that woman had some photos, we can take a glimpse at them. Are you Republican or Democrat?" Einar was being a bastard. He knew that Trixie had no idea what he meant, and she didn't.

"Republiwhat? Do I have to choose? Can't I just be a Repubocrat?"

"Ha, ha! Positively! You can be a Repubocrat." Einar's sarcasm and deep bellied laughter implied that Trixie's choice of parties was ridiculous. He knew that it was almost as ridiculous as the political rhetoric often spoken by Baldric's own priest, mayor, and any other figure valued with forced appreciation. Einar never once thought that combining both political parties could actually be genius.

"And what is your choice? Are you a republiwhatever or a something-o-crat?"

Just as Einar attempted to answer Trixie's question, Kluge briskly walked into the room and immediately interrupted the seemingly intelligent conversation that the twins attempted to hold.

"Well, well. How are you?" Kluge, obviously more comfortable in the confines of his personal office, approached the duo. His arms spread the width of the twins. Trixie continued to sit upright as any good-natured, innocent female should have done. Einar leaned back as far as he could. He hoped to melt into the floral pattern that was surrounding him and aimed to avoid the beaded oil and sweat nearly dripping off of the man's forehead.

To no avail, the lawyer did not decipher Einar's aversive body language and swooped his arms around the comfortably positioned twosome. As he leaned in, his breath reeked of the overwhelming blend of smoke and garlic. The obscene scent invaded the twins' noses. This caused Einar to sneeze uncontrollably and jolt his twin sitting next to him. Neither the sneeze nor Einar clearly seeping into the cushions stopped Kluge in his attempt to show human kindness. Kluge grabbed a hold of Lola's children. He hugged them a bit longer than necessary. It was creepy, especially for Einar who had read extensively about Kluge's relationship with Lola.

Kluge finally backed away from the twins. "It is time," he suggested, his hair now slightly disheveled from the invasive human contact, "to get down to business. Necessary business." He continued, "Now, you have to work to maintain the house. Shack or not. That means you have to have an income. Stable and consistent. When that happens, you will be free to live independently. Among yourselves, as members of society. Without an income, both of you will be placed under the guardianship of Ms. Smith." Kluge caught a glimpse of Trixie's confused look and added, "The living one."

At that moment, Kluge paid what seemed to be extra attention to Trixie. He looked at her and then looked her over. She immediately felt like intervening on his explanation and questioning him. The questioning, though, was not about the inappropriate glances. "Mr. Kluge, are you a something-o-crat or a Repubocrat?" Trixie's eyes had been naively opened to the political system. It interested her because of the funny words. She added, "I am a Repubocrat." And, she was certainly a proud Repubocrat.

Kluge took a moment to think about the question, and quite notably answered, "I, Miss Trixie, am an Independent." It was the most politically correct answer coming from a lawyer. He knew better than to choose sides without knowing the facts. He had little time to invest into the political system, and his lack of willingness to actually further the conversation showed this.

Without missing a beat, Kluge returned to the matter at hand. He held up a neatly packed manila folder, and spoke once again, "I have assembled this package." He placed the package in front of the twins. "For your benefit." As his fingers leafed through its contents, he explained, "It includes a copy of the most recent job listings, several applications for jobs within my family's business, the traveling circus, and a letter of recommendation from an esteemed Mr. Loki Kluge." Mr. Kluge now chuckled because he thought he was being witty by referring to himself in the third person. The real wit lay in his own belief that he deserved the adjective esteemed. The chuckling, which sounded more like a cackle in Einar's ears, made him even less so.

Kluge slid the folder toward the female twin and again continued, emphasizing his aspirations for the twins. "The traveling circus will be in town soon. I can interview you immediately…if you're interested."

Einar, with no interest in working for Kluge or any of the other Kluges, thought the man was full of himself and deviant by nature. Einar reacted to his own perception of Kluge and snatched the folder of miscellaneous papers off of the desk. Einar still thought that the stationary, mindless wooden structure was more revered than the man sitting behind it. "When must we report to you, concerning our success in the workforce?"

"You won't have to check in. No checks here." Plus, it is the law of the will that you will surrender to, not me, if you don't follow your mother's wishes. We all want what is best for everyone." Kluge reiterated the latter portion, "Best for everyone."

Trixie, understanding what was best for her at that moment, spoke, "Are we done? I am hungry." She may not have been the most educated and mentally adept person, but she was aware of her basic needs. Her basic need did not include an afternoon in the office that had the big pictures.

Kluge replied, raising his eyebrows in hopes to entice the twins one final time to join the circus, "Yes, you are finished. Any further questions?"

"Thanks." Einar, reciprocating an ingenuous glare that matched Kluge's raised brow, spoke as calmly as his temperament would allow. Einar had difficulty with the man's expectations. The twins were, after all, able to care for themselves without involvement from the law. Einar was going to do all that he could to prove this. He clenched the charitable folder and the bag of lunch gifted from the church cooks. "I have no further questions, so I surmise we will depart." Einar then wiped the glare from his face and turned to address his sibling, "Trix, I am famished; I know you are as well. We will have a nice, hearty lunch, deservedly so." Einar carefully enunciated the latter portion of his comment, as if to insinuate that Kluge was not deserving of a hearty lunch.

FOUR

Bewaring of the Delicacies

Einar dragged Trixie out of the courthouse. He firmly held onto the sack lunch and the folder as he and his sister stopped at the top of the marble stairs. While they lingered at the top, Einar took a large, masculine breath. Breathing in, he spoke, "This is what freedom smells like." It was a symbolic moment for the male twin. He was free from the constraints of his mother, his captor.

Trixie, who had no choice but to stop alongside Einar, took several small, silent breaths. She waited a moment until Einar was finished with his hefty puff of fresh air and then asked ever so politely, "What is freedom?" It could have been a contemplative, thoughtful question, but Trixie was inquiring, so it was not. Einar knew this.

He prepared a lengthy answer, but his thought process was interrupted when a gust of wind whisked by. Feeling the rush of the air caress his body, Einar, had hoped, although knowingly unrealistic, that the gust would have taken his lovely sister with it. She withstood nature's fury. That fleeting moment, Einar envisioned himself alone as he looked upon the gray tar splattered across the nearly vacant parking lot. Interrupted by a nudge, Einar looked next to him and realized that his sister had not miraculously been swept away. He pondered the answer his twin's question. Einar could have been an ass and meticulously outlined the events that led to his country's freedom, or he could have summarized the philosophy of free will. Yet, he knew that, just like in Kluge's office, she would pay the conversation forward to some unwilling participant. So, he chose to withhold a profound conversation about the meaning of freedom. He just responded, "This is freedom," and waved his free arm in the air.

Trixie did not accept the answer. This, and the allusion to abstract thought, was too broad for the girl. She questioned Einar again as they moved slowly, purposefully down the stairs. "Why are we free?" This question was more exact, and it took until the twins reached the natural, dirt ground for Einar to respond.

"Trix, Lola…momma, has died. She is gone. We are now capable to maneuver ourselves throughout the town without consequence."

"Why?" She could have been questioning whether or not they could actually move freely "without consequence", but Trixie was just questioning the death of her mother. It was a part of the grieving process.

Einar was certainly not utilizing the grieving process. Never once would he question his mother's death. Like he said, he was free. Seizing another few moments of silence, of freedom, Einar continued walking with Trixie. He soon spoke, "Lola cannot keep us at home anymore."

When alive, Lola did have leverage because she embedded enough fear into Einar that he felt obligated to watch over his sister and keep her safe at home. She would say, "Stay away from danger." Lola sketched a diabolic picture of society, one that would not kindly welcome Einar and Trixie. Perhaps the woman was paranoid, but she feared society's response to her children. It was her maternal instinct, as controversial as it may have been for the Smith household. This destroyed Einar's and his mother's relationship.

Much this relationship involved Lola coercing her son to abide by her one wish, avoiding the dangerous, outside world. She also strategically placed her diary in a place that Einar could find it.

The diary itself would keep Einar busy reading for hours. Unaware of Lola's ploy, Einar did have a slight, miniscule bit of respect for the woman who birthed him because she did, after all, give him some sort of life. Plus, he had a paternal-like worry for his sister, so he always followed Lola's one instruction. She would tell him, "They will stare at you." The "they" were the people of the town, and they would have stared, much like they did at the funeral. "They will steal you; take advantage of you." And, they, the people, might have. Now, without Lola, the twins would have to find out for themselves.

Einar glanced at his sister and suddenly empathized with the dead woman who he usually felt detest towards. He slightly understood his mother's past concerns. "I will take care of you." Although this statement was directed at Trixie, it was almost a reassurance to the deceased Lola that Einar would cautiously look after his sister, even in the event of an abduction.

Trixie agreed, "Okay." Trixie liked being taken care of. She accepted Einar's response, in part because she had forgotten what she was questioning all along. This was her one redeeming quality in Einar's eyes. At least she never held a grudge.

Devoid of grudges, questions, and answers, both twins enjoyed their first moment of their new lives, away from death and away from the chaos of life. They walked silently in the direction of the park only several feet away.

Once crossing the invisible barrier between the public walkway and the public park, Einar scoped out the benches to find a nice, clean one that faced away from the church and the law office. Einar did not want to be reminded of either place. Trixie would have preferred to look at the "pretty buildings", but she knew not to verbalize her desires. Einar was quite stubborn.

Aside from Einar and Trixie, few people were in the park that day, as all had returned to work after the ceremonial will reading. So, Einar and Trixie sat alone. They were exposed only to the forces of Mother Nature that happened to be quite civil at that moment. Einar opened the brown satchel that he had been carrying and pulled out a sandwich wrapped in waxed paper. He looked at the bag and then into the bag. His hand combed the remaining contents, an apple. He and his appendage hoped to find another, identical sandwich.

The lunch gifters must have been confused. They gave the twins only one lunch. Einar knew that he had to manage this misconception. "C'mon,"Trixie complained. She was hungry.

Without responding, Einar carefully unfolded the packaging and gave half of the sandwich to his sister. Her complaints and attention to her hunger were disturbed by the mysterious lunch meat and government cheese piled between two pieces of generic bread that she held in her hand. The bread had a slight crisp without ever being toasted, as to be expected. Trixie, though, wouldn't know this. She held the half sandwich and calmly whispered, "Dippy eggs." Clearly, there were no dippy eggs in her future, nor were there any in the bag.

Einar was concerned that the twin would not eat. He quickly replied, "The kind people did not give us dippy eggs, so you must eat what has been bestowed upon us." It was as much paternal guidance that the male could muster. And, luckily for the twins, the offering was not a brown bag lunch of dippy eggs, as that would have created quite an untidy lunch. Trixie adhered to Einar's request and did eat the sandwich as she looked heavenward to witness the flight patterns of the birds fluttering overhead. This calmed her frustration and diverted her attention from her wants. She ate in silence. Einar ate in silence.

When the twins were finished with the halves of the sandwich, Einar took a moment to digest and then grabbed the classifieds from the file folder given to him by Kluge. He uncrinkled the folds and began to read out loud, just to hold Trixie's attention. The birds had fluttered away, and the sandwich was gone. Einar spoke, "What career do you desire?" He was certainly motivated to prove to everyone: his dead mother, his aunt, and all of Baldric, that he and his sister could function as well as anyone else.

Remembering how unhappy she was with her lunch, although she ate it anyway, Trixie responded, "I want to make dippy eggs." She then spread her arms wide, as if to purport she would share her eggs with the world. The width of her span, although limited by the length of her arms, entirely invaded Einar's personal space on the park bench.

Einar avoided Trixie's intentional arm spasm and tried to quickly sway her attention from eggs, or any other restaurant work. He did not want the same chosen path as his mother. "Anything else? We could be…" Einar abruptly scanned over the usual ads for mechanics, secretaries, dishwashers, and escorts when one ad caught his eye, "an au pair." As a self-educator, Einar dabbled in a myriad of worldly languages, including Latin and French. He recognized the wanted position. It was one that would require the twins to escape Baldric and spend their days in the most fortunate of local, nearby towns. It was a town that prided itself on its local and monetarily significant potash extraction and lab-created potash production. Einar knew of the town and its source of prosperity, so the ad gripped his interest as he gripped the ad.

Trixie did not have a gripping interest in being an au pair. She immediately shook her head in disagreement while remnants of bread flew from the hidden places amongst her strands of hair, littering crumbs atop the shoulders of both the twins.

"We could frolic with children." Einar riddled his book smart vocabulary with more common speak for Trixie to understand. Au pair could be confusing for the female, who already thought that she and Einar were a pair. Aside from avoiding confusion, Einar also intended to interest his sister so that they too could live in potash enabled luxury and never be without soap or fertilizer again.

"I don't want to frrrrollllic. I want to..." And then, Trixie mimicked her best cook imitation borrowed from her deceased mother. Lola enjoyed cooking and baking in her own kitchen. To emulate this, the female twin took her pretend spatula, placed it into her imaginary pan on the makeshift stove that she created on her lap, and moved her arm, as if it were flipping eggs. Then, she buttered fictitious toast and placed the plate of illusion onto her brother's lap. "That is what I want to do; nothing else." It was evident that Trixie did not even understand the meaning of frolic.

"Play," Einar added.

"I don't want to play," Trixie retorted, making her opinion about being an "au pair" apparent.

Trying to ease his own tension that was building and the frustration that he had with his sister, Einar spoke. "As our dead mother as my witness, we will become employed, just not in a diner." Einar had an adverse reaction to following in his mother's footsteps, literally. He despised the scent of burnt grease and crusted salad dressing that followed her home. He was also witness to the weariness in her eyes after each day of work. Trixie never noticed. Consequently, Einar had to shun Trixie's wishes. It was his protective side that was hindering her.

Luckily for the Trixie and Einar, a troop of puppies soon distracted her. "Ohhh! Puppies!" She swung around as much as she could to watch a group of puppies handled by the only dog walker in the town. "Let's walk puppies." The career seemed to be simple enough for the twins, and they did not need any prior knowledge, except how to walk, which usually was not a daunting task for the duo, usually. Perhaps Trixie had just had an epiphany.

"You know that I despise animals." Einar's pride and expectations were slowly disappearing away with the wind that was picking up ever so slightly. Einar's lack of respect for the female twin because of her annoying anecdotes and lack of intelligent ideas were frustrating to him. In response to his sister's never-ending childishness, Einar abruptly placed the employment advertisements aside. He reached into the paper sack for the remainder of lunch. Einar caught hold of the apple and skimmed the bottom of the bag once more in hopes of finding a plastic knife or some other utensil to split the apple. Since Trixie was entranced by the puppies trotting and stooping around the park, Einar just bit into the bruise-ridden fruit.

"This is horrible." Einar held out the rotten apple, not wanting to smell nor see the fruit anymore. Before he could throw it out, Trixie grabbed the fruit. She consistently mocked her brother and his actions, except when those actions included reading or learning, two tasks Lola insisted that Trixie did not need. The girl was a female.

Trixie bit into the fruit, a delicacy of sorts because Lola prohibited that kind of sustenance in her home. The apple had too much Biblical meaning for the heathen. It was odd that the woman prepared to be buried in the church, but, of course, Lola did live a life of contradiction.

Watching Trixie rapaciously bite into the fruit, Einar waited for a response or a reaction. But, she continued eating. Einar was not going to keep her from any nutrients. He waited as patiently as he could for Trixie to devour the entire apple, except for the bit of a bite that he had eaten. While waiting, Einar did his best to clean up their luncheon. When his patience and duty subsided, Einar nudged Trixie, as she still held the core, off of the park bench. They stood, and the male wiped the lingering crumbs and bits of food off of his sister's body. Then, he extracted the core from her hand.

Einar was clearly frustrated.

"Where are we going?" Trixie, not yet ready to leave, questioned her brother.

"Home," Einar yelled back. He always seemed to arrange their travels, and Trixie always tried to obstruct her brother's plans. Perhaps this was because of her own natural fervor for even the most miniscule sense of freedom. She did not want the kind of freedom they found in the park; she wanted the kind of freedom that she could only obtain without her brother. That never happened.

"We are going home." Einar spoke those words with his most fatherly, stern voice. The force of the strong man was no match for his twin's smaller, more fragile physique.

"But I don't want to!" She looked at him with dismay but knew the look on his face was an unkind one as she caught a glimpse of his furrowed brow. She continued on in silence, just as Einar had hoped. And, Einar was silently frustrated by his inability to agree with Trixie's choice of employment. The task of finding a job that both the twins would enjoy had been thwarted, and his lunch that should have eased his tension had been ruined by the inedible apple. He felt empty.

FIVE

They Shall Return Once More

For the first time since their mother's funeral, the twins returned to their home. It was a makeshift shack devoid of any maternal tenderness. A mist of invisible dust smothered their faces and their minds when they entered. An air of doom still hovered throughout the kitchen. It was a dark, sterile space, yet Trixie still stumbled over Einar's feet. The force of Einar's reach to grope the wall to find the light switch and unmask the darkness kept Trixie from hitting the floor.

With the suggestion of the on switch, the kitchen light hanging over the faux marble counter of demise, flickered several times until it could bear the sparks of electricity traveling through its veins. Once established, the light hanging above the countertop glimmered its rays upon a basket of quinces. Aside from the bowl of fruit, the span of the reproduced stone was empty, leaving only memories of a once cluttered death trap.

"Whew! It smells like pneumonia." Trixie was the first to recognize the awkward scent.

"Well, that is not possible, since no one in this house has suffered from that annoying disease. You must mean ammonia." Einar, of course, smelled it the moment Trixie exclaimed her opinion of the awful smell. It was a simple mistake for the simple minded girl, although she should have had, since she was well past childhood age, the mind of a woman.

"The cleaning stuff, that's what I mean." Trixie, for the first time, seemed bothered by her brother's correction. He had known all along what she meant, and she knew it.

Making their way from the kitchen to the dining room, the twins prowled together across the linoleum. Einar took caution in his steps. He worried that they too could slip and fall, just like Lola. He focused on the table that stood just steps away. It could serve as a buffer if they happened to fall. His concern was senseless, as the arid flooring only added resistance to their footing as they approached the plastic dinette set. It was a lavish ensemble for the home once kept by Lola.

After denouncing Trixie's desires for employment earlier, Einar, having felt the strange emotion of guilt, attempted to coerce her to help him in his prolific quest to find a career or even just a job. "Will you guide me in finding suitable employment?" While awaiting an answer, he frisked the contents of his shoulder bag filled with the necessary information kindly given to him by Kluge. Einar still preferred to refer to the helpful man as "an idiot".

Trixie, oblivious to the task Einar was about to undertake, ignored her brother's questioning and began a more important endeavor—pleasing the audience in her mind with her own concerto as she sat on the plastic bench. She never thought to answer Einar's question.

Realizing that his sister was not going to respond, Einar meticulously placed all the given documents in a particular order. His orchestrated act was interrupted every so often by some simple hums that invaded his right ear due to his sister's abnormal proximity.

"Please quiet down," Einar suggested. He was not aware that creating an ambiance was how Trixie intended to help with her brother's undertaking.

"Quiet what?" Trixie questioned her sibling.

"Never mind," Einar soon retorted.

Trixie continued entertaining her mind, and Einar continued his more realistic expedition. He searched the ads and made a list of feasible employment options. This only took several minutes. When Einar had a full list of appropriate, available jobs, he infringed on Trixie's musical endeavors once again. "Here, peruse this list." Einar hoped for his sister's approval. He brushed the checklist to the edge of the table. Patiently, he waited for her response.

Trixie took a moment to survey the components of the paper. Her eyes met the page, and it would have only been a matter of time before what was written on the page would have traveled through the depths of her eyes into the shallowness of her brain. If this manifestation took place, Trixie would have thoroughly read the paper. But, she did not.

When her eyes removed themselves from the paper that Einar so cautiously, yet efficiently, prepared, Trixie looked to the ceiling as if deep in thought; she wasn't. Her eyes jutted from the awning of the light fixture and then to the framed picture of her family, which had become two thirds of what it once was.

"So, what do you suppose?"

"It's fine." Trixie responded out of silent protest to the annoying pestering. Although she never actually read the paper that was forced in front of her, she agreed to the list anyway.

"Well, I will commence the work. We will need a resumé, as suggested by Kluge, and it says here," Einar held up a document bulleted with a myriad of important notes to remind the twins as to how the process of entering the workforce worked. He continued, "At least one more letter of recommendation. Who do you suggest write that?" Obviously vying for further involvement from Trixie to ensure that she would cease her incessant humming and any other incessant, annoying behavior, Einar attempted to enable her. He was used to never being apart from his sister and always found ways to distract her as much as she found ways to distract herself.

"Aunt Evelyn." Trixie's response was due to the fact that Aunt Evelyn was perhaps the only person she actually knew.

Einar did not at all find the drunken, selfish woman favorable, yet he agreed with Trixie's suggestion. "Just call Aunt Evelyn," Einar commanded as he pushed the landline phone that was a fixture on the dining table toward the twin. "I will begin creating the resumé," he added.

"Sure," Trixie agreed. She would never protest work that included pushing buttons and talking into a funny looking sound receptacle.

She would have called her aunt immediately, but Trixie waited until Einar was finished rustling the papers and setting up the antique Remington. The typewriter was an appliance that Lola had often used to write anonymous love letters to anonymous criminals in the local jail. Einar, concerned about the demented use of the typewriter, prepared himself and the ancient form of technology by wiping his fingers and the keys with rubbing alcohol that he found at the bottom of his bag. It was an unsuccessful attempt to remove the soiled memories. Because she thought that cleanliness was also necessary to begin her task, Trixie did the same with the phone. It was not at all because she was aware of Lola's devious excursions with that device.

When all was disinfected, except Einar's remembrances of his mother, the twins began their roles in an effort to find a reputable career. Einar typed the necessary document one poke at a time with pudgy fingers that lapped along the neighboring keys of the ones he opted to press, and Trixie dialed the aunt's number, pecking the numbers ever so carefully with her slender digits. She cautiously read the tiny shred of paper tattooed with the phone number that Einar slid to her. This time, she was willing to read the writing, and the pecking was an obvious sign.

Although Trixie was capable of entering the correct number

into the phone, she was not triumphant in her endeavor, since Aunt Evelyn did not answer the call. Trixie was forced to leave a message. She then aborted any other attempt to fulfill her duty, although she spent many minutes staring at the phone, tempting it to ring. It did not, but the click of the typewriter keys kept the twin positioned at the table. Restlessness did not creep upon the twin until the clicking ceased. And just as she was about to endlessly bother her brother for the rest of the evening, her attention turned to the kitchen when she heard several short raps upon the door.

The twins had rarely heard the sound of knocking. Few people ever visited the home that sat back from the main road. The twins had become mere legends in the town after they were confined for so many years. The people of Baldric gave up on their insatiable desire to menace the family, except for that rude neighbor of theirs. The shack, with its small stature that was hidden by a vast array of thickets and lengthened weeds, aided in sheltering the home and the twins from any nuisances, except, again, from the nuisance of the neighbor. Consequently, the knock startled both inhabitants of the home, and Einar rose and stood alongside Trixie who was trying to hide herself from the unknown that existed beyond the front door that was decorated with a welcoming wreath, as if it welcomed anyone.

"Who is it?" Einar questioned.

Einar waited, only to eavesdrop on the quaint conversation of silence.

"Is anyone present?" He questioned again.

A muted hush, except for the heavy breathing that Trixie guided down Einar's neck, invaded the house. She held onto him for comfort and security. She was clearly frightened.

Without another word, Einar slowly snuck toward the door. He led Trixie, whose grip was turning more and more tight, nearer the exterior door. As the duo stepped, the wooden planks that surrounded the doorway creaked of wear and tear. It was a fitting ambiance for the situation, and the mysterious horror of an uninvited visitor caught them off guard and terrified them, especially the more feminine of the twins, namely Trixie.

Before Einar opened the door, he knocked several times and waited for any mimic of the same. There was none, so slowly he opened it. His heart pounded loudly enough for his twin to hear. Trixie stood silently and listened to the repetitive poundings that Einar's heart offered. Unwilling to advance past the barrier between the door and the outside, Trixie held onto Einar's arm and allowed him to advance only enough to bend down and inspect the entranceway.

The inspection was deemed successful as soon as Einar spotted a box labeled "Einar and Trixie Smith". It was strategically placed off to the side of the pathway where the light of the moon beamed down in the otherwise deep, dark blackness. Before picking up the package to examine its contents, Einar, still attached to Trixie, scanned the area for any sign of life. There was none except for the perpetual heavy breathing of his sister. His neck was warm from her fear, yet a faint breeze cooled him as he leaned down to pick up the drop off. As quickly as he scooped up the parcel, he slammed the door and guided Trixie back to the kitchen table. There they, having never seen a real package addressed to them, sat for several minutes entranced by the small, brown box.

"We should open this," Einar whispered, as if the unknown visitor was eavesdropping on their conversation. After he spoke, Einar's excitement and curiosity were rising. "We will open this and view the innards." Einar poked his sister as he spoke.

Trixie, still awed at the package that had her name attached to it, was unable to respond, and oddly, not once did she think that he meant to open her belly. She was too mesmerized, so Einar, without the cooperation of his twin, began to open the mysteriousness that sat upon the table. Moving it closer, he disassembled the taping that kept its contents protected from the elements of the outer world. With the strips of tape and bits of box scattered about, Trixie, eventually deciding to assist her brother, pulled the flaps open. Einar reached in and grabbed what seemed to be a folded paper contained within a secure envelope.

Much more inquisitive than moments prior, Trixie offered her support even more. "Open it; open it," she said as she clapped her hands. Then she inquired, "What does it say?"

Einar couldn't respond immediately. With all of the invasive tearing and ripping, the envelope scratched and sliced his finger as it slid through the envelope. It stalled his movement to investigate the contents, but within moments, Einar was able to hold his injured pointer off to the side and use his other hand to peel the contents from the contained envelope that had become splotched with beads of blood. As the thin piece of paper was smoothed out and the red smears dried, Einar began to read. He unknowingly copied the tone of the speaker from earlier in the day; he raised his voice just like Kluge. This time, though, it did not sound like poor, deceased Lola Smith. "Dear Smith twins, Gertrude Sconch cordially invites you to become an employee of Baldric Theater for its production of "Modern Times". The silent film will be portrayed as a musical atop the fabulous Baldric Theater stage. If interested, please report to the theater tomorrow, promptly at noon."

"Does that mean…"Trixie could not make out the rest of her question before Einar interrupted her.

"We, Trix, are going to have a job at the theater."

Becoming a working man by portraying a working man during the height of capitalism was more than Einar could have ever hoped for. He wanted so much to be an integral part of the American dream. Einar's excitement, along with the letter that meant what it conveyed, could not unveil the devastating opinions that Lola had of the theater. Einar knew that she had shunned the theater. She thought it was a soiled, unrealistic, sinful place. But, he had often thought those were appropriate adjectives to describe her.

SIX

Commencing an Investment

Mid morning the next day, the twins, clad in periwinkle suiting, made their way towards the theater. An intricately drawn map that was detailed with erased pencil markings and scribbles guided the twins' travels. Even though the map was overly cluttered with barely visible, extraneous markings, Einar methodically followed the darkest hued of the marks; this was how, after they trekked across the town along the cracked sidewalks, Einar and Trixie finally reached their destination.

"We are approaching our destination," Einar cautiously validated, after referencing the map one final time.

The twins slowed their pace and entered through the metal encasing that surrounded the yard of the theater, which was a drab, cement building.

As Einar and Trixie advanced toward the large, hollow, aluminum door, Einar spotted a small plaque, infused into a large, red brick, scripted with the word: THEATER. It was the twin's final affirmation that he and his sister were in the right place.

The male twin took a moment to sigh and realize that he was content, much to his dead mother's dismay, to take Trixie beyond the park, beyond the church, beyond Kluge's office, and beyond the confines of a shack of a home nestled deep amid natural foliage. While Einar was reflecting on the freedom that he and his sister had been introduced to, Trixie was reflecting on why the clouds had become so dark, and her prod toward the door interrupted Einar's thoughts. Escaping the hint of rain, the twins entered the theater for the first time ever.

After walking briskly through the dark foyer, which was usually-just not that day- lit by sets of gaudy, colorful Christmas lights, Einar guided Trixie through the building. He wasn't sure where they were going, but they continued to go anyhow. They exited the lobby, walked past the restrooms, and peeked through the black curtains that led to the seating area. Einar decided to continue. Being forced by the natural gravitational pull of the slope, Einar and Trixie walked down the inside aisle-way. Their dark shadows, lit by the wall sconces along the outside aisles, arrived at the stage moments earlier than they did.

Not knowing what to do next, Einar and Trixie stood at the foot of the stage and watched an array of eager puppets practicing one of the various dance numbers. Along with the dancing came the demands. "And uno, and dos, and tres. No, no, no! You, you in the back, you are off, off beat. Try it again." The masculine female (or feminine male) who spoke English instructions that were sprinkled with random Spanish words, spoken with a clear American accent, reiterated the directions for the puppets. The person said nothing to the twins who were still standing behind in front of the stage, watching.

The asexual director was Gertrude Sconch. When Gertrude looked upon the stage, the indistinguishably gendered director saw something much different than what the twins had witnessed. They saw excitement; they saw beauty. Gertrude did not. As creator, director, and choreographer, the she-male always deemed, "Practice, practice, practice makes perfect. Perfecto." The movements of the unenthusiastic cast of marionettes were not "perfecto". What made the sight even worse for Gertrude was the crippled puppet in the back row. Although it attempted to mirror the drudgery of being a member of the general workforce, the disability deterred the puppet from actually following Gertrude's directives. Gertrude was well aware. Thus, the brutal work continued.

As Einar looked upon the stage, he saw the wooden dolls, the strings hanging from the rafters, and the monkey sitting atop the director's shoulder. From Einar's vantage point, Gertrude did look like a woman, even if she did command like a man. Einar continued watching the spectacular, and he knew that the inanimate objects could not be perfect, as they were, well, inanimate. The mistakes did not bother him; the commands did not distract him. It was all still exciting and beauteous.

Unaware of the unrealistic expectations and the quiet observers, Gertrude continued ranting. Trixie watched the small puppets bounce back and forth and bob their heads in a myriad of attempts to prove their rhythmic capabilities. Trixie saw the marionettes winking at her every time they nodded. She felt special, and her eyes were glued to the wooden dancers in her own attempt to mentally memorize their movements. This was a special moment and a new experience. Trixie enjoyed this.

The practice seemed to be successful to the twins, even if some of the puppets unintentionally stalled their movements and were unable to keep up with the beat. As a result, the marionettes did not please the cast, the crew, the director, or the pet monkey still atop the director's shoulders. Even the animal knew more about theater than the twins. It shielded its eyes from the dastardly sight. As the monkey was showing its disappointment for the train-wreck of a production, Gertrude shouted opinions in a clearly maddened tone, "No, no, no!" The practice was halted for an indeterminate amount of time. This was clear after Gertrude yelled, "Cinco! Diez! Whatever." And then, all was quiet. There were no thumps of the wood bashing against the stage floor, no yelling, no music blaring from the speakers just to be halted later by a screech. Silence replaced it all, briefly.

Turning around, the director interrupted the silence. "Who

are you?" As Gertrude caught the attention of the twins, the laser eyes of the director darted toward Trixie and Einar. The eyes overlooked the twins and then looked over the twins, who were approaching the director ever so cautiously. As they neared, it became clear, at least to Einar, that Gertrude was a hermaphrodite.

Not expecting such a sight, Einar was caught off guard. Gertrude had all of the facial characteristics of a man, the voice of a man, the breast of a woman, and the dress of a woman. Einar took a moment to genderize the director and concluded that Gertrude was more man than woman. This whole process was terribly distracting for Einar, but he soon prepared to address the person known as Gertrude. He answered the question asked of him previously. "We, um, sir, are Einar and Trixie Smith. We are here to inquire about the opportunity for employment." As unlikely as it was, Einar was losing his fluency and fluidity of speech. He was startled, especially by the forcefulness of the man, as was Trixie who was still shaken by the abrupt welcoming.

"Opportunity? You've been given the chance of a lifetime! El ensueno. It's not a simple, measly opportunity." Gertrude peered over his shoulder, the one free from any primate, to ensure that the marionettes were still lifeless. They were. Content, the hermaphrodite turned around once more and crooked his neck to glare at the twins. The twins watched as Gertrude nearly penetrated their souls with his eyes. His concentration was broken when the monkey jumped and sat at the feet of the twins. For a man who often wore dresses and other feminine garb, Gertrude, other than his outer appearance, had neither the pleasantries nor the tact of a woman. His voice was stern and his actions were harsh. Based on what everyone witnessed in the theater that day, Gertrude Sconch was in dire need of real, true thespians, yet his approach suggested something different. "The show must go on. Make it brief."

"Well sir, um, ma'am," Einar attempted to smooth over the situation with a proper addressing when he was interrupted.

"Me llamo es Mzzz. Gertrude," Gertrude corrected while emphasizing the Mzzz. of his name. He stood as upright and as proud of his gender-confused identity as possible. His voice thundered through the empty area.

Instead of maintaining the conversation, Einar drew his and Trixie's limited credentials from the manila folder that he had been carrying with him since the day before. Einar reached his hand over the stage and handed the information, including the letter, to Gertrude. After further inspection, Einar was not convinced that it was a she or even a Mzzz.

Gertrude slouched down and snatched the letter and other pieces of paper that Einar handed to him. He then, using his most lady-like manners, found a seat at the edge of the stage and crossed his legs. He affixed his reading monocle and cautiously read the letter that he had personally prepared and hand-delivered shortly after hearing about the genetic wonders of Baldric. And, although the proof of the twin's existence was in their presence that day, Gertrude wanted to ensure them that he meant business. Still attentive to the papers, Gertrude spoke, "Do you have reliable transportation?"

"Yes," Einar answered. He considered his own legs a source of reliable transportation.

"Are you willing to begin your work day early in the morning and end late in the evening?" He asked. These questions were clearly derived from Interviewing 101. Actually, Gertrude had little formal training in this aspect of his job, so he just did what he saw in the movies.

"Yes," Einar answered.

"Is the law looking for you?" Gertrude asked.

"Um, uh, no," Einar responded. He was sure that Kluge mentioned something about the law, but he just couldn't recall that information, and in turn, could not confidently answer the question. Einar then shrugged another answer in an "I don't know" kind of way; Trixie shrugged simultaneously with him. Obviously, Einar was not necessarily concerned with the law, or the law with Einar.

"Moving on, do you want this job?" Gertrude asked. He then stated, "This is an opportunity of a lifetime."

"Oh, sir, yes! More than ever! I, we, are able and willing to take on an endeavor such as this, this opportunity of a lifetime," Einar enthusiastically answered. He was perhaps a bit too enthusiastic. Einar would have agreed to any job for himself and his sister, except that of a diner worker or a pet walker. Of course, those were both Trixie's ideas.

"Do you appreciate the arts?" Gertrude asked, interrupting the excitement.

"What do you mean?" Einar was confused by the question. Einar was also clearly incorrect in questioning the questioner.

"Wrong!" Gertrude exclaimed. Of all of the inquiries, the latest should have been the most quickly answered. The arts, of course, should always be appreciated. Einar did not understand this.

"I didn't answer!" Einar exclaimed in response.

"The answer is clear, obvious; it is 'yes', 'si'!" Gertrude was out of questions for the time being, so he turned his attention to the letter. He readjusted his reading glass and carefully read. After thorough inspection, he deemed it authentic. His eyes lifted to meet those of Trixie's. He spoke again, "Hey missy, you want a job here?"

Trixie, although excited by her chance to speak, was also slightly confused and angry about Gertrude's mistake. "I am not Missy!"

"Yes!" Gertrude was taunting the girl with an answer.

Trixie was still confused about the name calling. "No, it's not

Missy; it's Trixie."

"I mean, the answer, it should be 'Yes!'"

"Then, yes, but I," Trixie retorted. She became quite confident in herself and what she knew to be true, so she continued, "I am not Missy; I am Trixie."

Gertrude made himself very clear, "You are who I say you are!" He then continued, in a less than volatile manner. "Well, ahora, you are my employees!" Gertrude raised his eyes from the paperwork and used his monocle to survey the twins as if they were documents of their own. "Begin tomorrow morning. Now vamos!" Gertrude waved his hands in a "get moving" kind of way. The nonverbal cues were clear.

This brief inquisition startled Einar who had subconsciously hoped for more of a challenge in his efforts to enter the workforce. The whole idea of business and employment, in his eyes, meant competition. Even with all of the questioning, he figured the process would be more tedious and worrisome. The Spanish speaking man made it much less so.

SEVEN

Leading to Affecting Resentment

The next morning, after the brief inquisition with Gertrude, the newly employed twins awoke because of the intrusive beeping sound of the alarm clock that Einar placed next to his ear. He found the device the night before next to his mother's bed. Waking first, Einar was unaccustomed to such an obnoxious shrieking sound that ricocheted across the room so early in the morning. His eyes eventually opened, just as a hint of moonshine crept through the window and intoxicated them. This morning routine was a brief shock to the twin who was used to sleeping so soundly after many years of sharing such close quarters with another human, his sister. Einar sat up and wiped his sleep-encrusted eyes. He then shook Trixie, who was an even deeper sleeper, in an attempt to wake her from her content slumber. She turned with a smirk and had to take a moment to examine her reality, the bed, the darkness, and her brother poking her right arm. Within moments, though, the girl sat up. Einar then pushed her off of the bed. He rolled off following her.

"Dawn will arrive at any moment. We must make a positive first impression on our inaugural day of work." Einar whispered into Trixie's ear as she remained on the floor after the sudden roll off of the bed.

Trixie then questioned, "Who is Dawn?" Trixie was cognizant enough to ask questions, although her questions lacked any intellectual integrity.

With no time to mock his sister, Einar quickly answered, "The morning."

"Oh, oh yeah, the sun." Trixie soon realized her mistake and comprehended nearly the entirety of Einar's statement; her agreement proved this.

"We must prepare for our full day of work."

Trixie nodded her head, in recognition to Einar's statement. She was, at least, mentally prepared. Of course, her idea of work included watching a bunch of wooden dolls dance about and make horrible clunking sounds atop the stage. That was what she did the day prior; that is what she expected to do that day. On the other hand, Einar did not assume anything of the sort, and although he and his sister may have had misconceptions about work, they were both confident and enthusiastic. Einar was receptive to the idea that after thirty years, he was going to experience life.

Aside from the anticipated mental preparation that the twins needed for the day, they also spent many minutes physically preparing for the day. This included the appropriate showering and dressing. These were tasks that most members of the workforce needed to accomplish. When the twins were content with their outfitting and their mental states (as determined by Einar), they headed on their way to the theater.

The twins' daybreak eagerness lasted all the way through the fields of dandelions and lengthy weeds onto the pavement upon which they pounded to arrive at their destination, their fate. The softness of the rain soaked ground softened their steps as they walked onto the theater yard. Aside from the previous presence of rain, the theater had never looked so intriguing. The gray cinder block masked a perpetually brighter place. It was a place of hopes and of dreams, although it had always been a prohibited place for the twins. Their existence was being solidified by their newfound employment outside of the confines of their home.

The twins anxiously, hand in hand, skipped along the path to the entrance. The skipping was awkward as the duo's legs rubbed together and caused a sound of rustling cloth. The swish, swish of their pants, one leg brushing against the other, coincided with every jaunt. The sound ceased as the twins approached the door and stopped, for just a moment, to take in the sights.

"Remember this," Einar suggested.

"Remember what?" Trixie responded. She kind of knew, though, that this moment was special.

Baldric sky was beautiful first thing in the morning, and it was a sight and a moment that neither Einar nor Trixie wanted to forget. The rise of Kluge's tower grabbed the sunlight, allowing it to bounce off of the windows and shed light upon the otherwise dismal town. As the two pairs of eyes circumvented the display of the town, the twins soon focused their attention on the metal doors that both stood slightly ajar. The doors reflected the rays of the early morning sun and Kluge's office building. With a slight pull, Einar, with Trixie's help, was able to open the doors enough to unveil the theater at rest. It was a serene vision, although not as serene as the twins had witnessed moments earlier. After following the runner into the theater area, they scanned the vast span of empty seats and stage shielded by a velveteen curtain. Everything was motionless. Einar determined that the theater was not as dismal of a place as Lola determined. Of course, the dimmed lights and faint smell of overwork could have countered this thought.

The dark theater was silent, and behind the twins, the metal door closed with a thud and trapped the still air. The reverberations lasted several moments, and then it was silent again. With limited distractions, Trixie looked around the theater and spotted the dolls scattered among the front row of seating. With haste, she pulled Einar in the direction of the marionettes. Gertrude, aware of the twins' arrival by the echoes from the entrance, stepped from the lifeless curtain and spoke, as if entirely understanding Trixie's intentions. "Don't touch the puppets. Las manos lejos."

Fearing that Trixie did not understand or hear his request, Gertrude rushed to the dolls' aid. He smoothed the tousled pieces of his hair and then approached one of the dolls and did the same in an attempt to also mitigate his reproach until he spoke again. "Have a seat," he insisted, and then he stated an obvious, English request, "an empty one."

Einar, not noticing any empty, suitable seating near Gertrude, turned toward the stage. Trixie followed his pursuit, and they both climbed up to position themselves on the edge. Sitting snugly next to one another, they awaited the next set of instructions. The monkey, a necessary accessory for Gertrude, followed the instructions also and took a seat in the front row of the theater in a seat that Einar and Trixie bypassed.

"This is a privileged establishment. Understand? Comprendes?" Gertrude did not wait for a response as he continued. "You'll become part of it. You'll be expected to pay homage to all who've come before you. You'll be paid for your efforts. Con mucho dinero. The real pay is the pride you earn as a part of this historical plateau." Gertrude gushed his opinion of theatrical grandeur as he paced back and forth in front of the twins.

As soon as Gertrude paused, Einar interrupted Gertrude's moment of silence. "Do we need formal training?" He questioned. He preferred asking the questions. Einar probably should have inquired about the formalities of the job the day prior but became too distracted by the "chance of a lifetime" and the oddly smelling monkey.

"Absolutely not. You'll be stars, if you heed my instructions. How does that make you feel?" Gertrude turned toward Trixie. He hoped that if he drew her into his plan, nothing could stop in his path toward entertainment domination in a dwindling field.

The theater was something that he found difficult success in year after year. Limited time, limited budgets, and limited ideas destroyed the theater. Plus, the ever popular moving pictures became the theater's nemesis. So, his plan to emulate the movies was his best ploy to entertain an attention span deprived society. Plus, he was aware that if he utilized the twins appropriately, Baldric would have many more theater goers. Gertrude was desperate for a solution, and the twins were his answer. He pondered this as he taunted Trixie for a response.

Trixie did respond appropriately. "Yes, a star, I would like to be a star." Knowing that stars were shiny and pretty, Trixie suddenly felt less intimidated by the man called Gertrude.

Since Gertrude grasped the girl's attention, he continued, speaking more seriously than he did before. "I will dictate your movements, your actions, and even your thoughts. A theater production is an intricate endeavor, and you have to treat it like a well-oiled machine, like any job where workers rely on each other. You must rely on me. Never, nunca, question me, and always do as I say. If you can't produce, you don't earn pay. No dinero." Gertrude's speech was poignant and clear, at least the English part was clear.

Finished with his formal introduction to the theater, Gertrude slowed his pace to a stop and glared at the twins. He was actually just deep in thought. "Now, ahora…" he paused, holding Einar's and Trixie's attention with his silence. Eventually, he spoke again, "Take center stage. Before you dare imitate the art, the fine art of theater, bellas artes, you must have an appropriate introduction." After Einar and Trixie remained in their seated positions moments too long to appease the director, Gertrude shouted, "Ahora!" Trixie did not know what the word ahora meant, like several of the other words that Gertrude had used in their brief two-day exchange, but Gertrude's tonnage alerted her to his temperament. He meant business. Einar, on the other hand was not distracted by

Gertrude's tone, as he was just thankful that Gertrude's continuous demands in Spanish would help the male twin add another language to his repertoire.

Eventually abiding to Gertrude's instruction, both twins stood simultaneously and took center stage, the spot with the large masking tape x. They stood, and a flood of bright light nearly blinded them. It was streaming from a dark room in the back of the theater. Then, lights shone brightly from the fixtures above the stage. Gertrude ordered them again. "Don't move." They didn't. And, just when the standing became monotonous and tiresome, a short man, strapped with a flexible measuring tape, pulled up a chair and stood upon it. He didn't speak to the twins, although he did tip his newsboy cap to acknowledge them; the twins didn't speak to him, nor did they acknowledge him. This was merely because Gertrude had, moments earlier, shouted, "Don't speak. Don't move." They did neither, although the non-speaking proved difficult for the girl. She quietly giggled every time the man brushed his miniature hand across her arm, and then her bosom, and eventually her leg. Gertrude said nothing about not giggling. Plus, Trixie liked the feeling. The little man did not enjoy it as much—Einar and Trixie were just not his type.

The midget had no difficulty marking the measurements of the twins, even if it took much longer than if a normal sized human would have been employed for the task. As the small man made measurements of the twins, the monkey sat in the front row. The latter of the two was distracted by a myriad of colored pencils and a large piece of paper. It was fervently making appropriate markings on the once blank drawing tablet that it held in its lap. Drawing was quite an esoteric skill for the primate. Everyone and everything had a role in the theater.

Utilizing more time than necessary, with one final swoop of the tape around the twins' midsection, three sections at a time, the small man finished his duty, stepped off of the chair, and vanished into the back. The monkey was still working, so Gertrude instructed the twins "Remain, still. No giggling this time. We have a serious production to undertake."

The serious undertaking for the day included measurements for wardrobe and a portrait for the marquee. Gertrude had, with the little man and the monkey, created an unlikely conglomerate for himself and his business. For this, he was a genius, and while the genius was standing in front of the stage and framing the twins' faces with his fingers, the beaded sweat on Einar's and Trixie's foreheads became increasingly profound. The sweat dripped and amassed on the wooden boards upon which their feet stood. The image was becoming less pleasing for the monkey. By the time a clear puddle formed, and the monkey seemed less interested in the artistry of drawing, Gertrude finally ended the session. "Enough! Suficiente!"

The streaming spotlight soon trickled to a glimmer, luring only the dust moseying throughout the air. It was perfect timing, as the monkey had lost all attentiveness to the portrait. This disinterest turned tragic as the monkey began to throw all the tangible items that spread within his reach and then watched the aforementioned items flutter through the air, along with shreds of paper that it had shredded moments earlier. Eventually, it was because of the brash of flying colored pencils and floating bits of blank confetti that the workplace had become hazardous. Thus, the workday was terminated much sooner than Einar and Trixie anticipated.

EIGHT

A Foretelling, Bizarre Episode

Einar's and Trixie's first day of work was deceiving. As the week progressed, the days became longer, the monkey became less distracting, and the midget, the one with the small, tickling fingers, was nowhere to be found. The twins' duties, which seemed more robotic than artistic, were beyond their expectations, especially considering the appeal of the profession itself. They worked long days that entailed following directives, listening to respectable berating and interminable expletives, and eventually learning an odd series of movements that Gertrude labeled as "dance steps". It was an American sweat shop, except the twins were not only mentally abused and poorly paid (as this was undetermined). Their bodies, hued with blue, black, and red markings, had suffered tremendously as well. Although they were used to moving simultaneously, the twins were not especially cognizant of their inability to actually have any skill at dance.

Relief finally arrived when the twins prepared for the final work day of the week. The relief that they clenched onto was the allure of real monetary bills, and for Trixie's sake, some shiny coinage. The elusive appeal of payday was the only encouragement for the twins to roll out of bed and assume their roles in the theater. Their hard, daunting work was supposedly going to be duly compensated.

"Trix, you must get out of bed. If we do not arrive on time, we will not receive our earnings. And through all of our strife, we are entitled to our theatrical indemnity."

They were entitled to some indemnity, although Trixie was unsure as to what that was. She had little energy to question it and just routinely readied for the day with Einar alongside her. They were pursuing the American dream.

When they exited their home, which had become quite a serene lovely place without Lola and without Gertrude, the twins salvaged as much energy as possible by trekking to the nearest bus stop and waiting like the other less than eager members of the workforce. Both twins understood that as their work load had increased throughout the week, and so did their humbling need to employ public transportation. Energy and time could be salvaged in Einar's nearly brilliant idea to be transported by bus, even if Trixie, every time she stepped onto the bus, became increasingly annoying and childish. With every bump and every halt, Trixie found amusement. She found public transportation to be quite appealing.

By this day, the appeal of the bus had worn off, and Trixie's giggles and child-like behavior ceased. Both Einar and Trixie shuddered at the thought of seeing Gertrude raise his arms that were flooded by his ornate mumu and taunt the oscillating fans that did little to ventilate the dark room of the theater. By this day, the murmuring voices of the bus did little to drown out the memories of Gertrude shouting and clapping. Work was certainly paying its toll as neither Einar nor Trixie even noticed the attention afforded them on the bus that day. The ride became increasingly crowded; the stares had never been so distinct. And, Einar had never lacked so much perception, although he did note, "This idea of work is…" For a moment, he could not think of the words, but he eventually continued, "cluttering my thoughts."

As soon as he noted his mental confusion, the bus stopped, and the twins stepped onto the hard concrete, the theater within their sights and apprehension on their minds. They left behind the incessant ogles and followed the gray, sectioned cement that led them to the simple square box where they spent most of their time. Opening the door, Einar found the theater to be much less tranquil than he had once thought. The memories of the past week had been etched into Einar's collection of memories, and he nearly winced as he walked through the barrier from the outside world. Trixie, with no thoughts and few memories, just stumbled alongside him. Barely keeping her eyes open, she was thankful, just that once, that Einar led her in the correct direction.

"Welcome, welcome, welcome," Gertrude welcomed the twins that morning. He was surprisingly delighted and thoroughly focused on the English language. The monkey, also content to see the twins' arrival, aped the hermaphrodite by clapping its hands once the twins entered. The director then transitioned his welcomes into demands that the twins were so used to hearing, "Let's go; let's go; let's go. Puppets get ready. Ahora! Ahora!" Gertrude was overly enthusiastic and confident and finally tapped into his second nature tongue.

Trixie was unsure whether Gertrude was referring to her or Einar, or the puppets, with his directives, so she figured he was uncertain of the differences; the puppets practiced much more sophisticated movements. Gertrude actually wasn't ambivalent and did motion to all as if they were all mere puppets upon his stage; they were.

The twins approached the stage as directed. Concurrently, all six of the puppets, including the miraculously healed cripple, whose leg was sanded down to its natural hue and showed only a hint of scarring from the dried glue leaking from its joints, slowly fell from the rafters above the platform.

"Twins, find your mark. Puppets, find yours." Gertrude distinguished between the two. He was pleased that his plans were coming to fruition and his voice, in all its civility, just for a moment, reflected that. Gertrude then rushed the workers, urging them, in a much less civilized manner, to speed along. "Hurry, hurry. Rapido, rapido. Time is money. Dinero. Let's go." He tapped his foot and waited impatiently, and when all was settled, he cued the music, "And uno, dos, music, I need mus..." The demand was interrupted by the music blaring through the speakers. The puppets danced as they were told, and the workday began and continued just like any other. They practiced, practiced, and practiced because practice made "perfecto".

Actually hours into the day, shortly after the third practice of the first act commenced, the hollow metal door opened and allowed a ray of light, guided by the aisle, to cut through the darkness. The apparition, whose figure was much larger than the monkey but smaller than the hermaphrodite, appeared and stood at the open door for several seconds.

The twins soon noticed the figure shuffling to the forefront and becoming much less of an apparition and more of a blood and flesh human. While watching the visitor maneuver down the aisle, Trixie became increasingly distracted by the possibly intoxicated figure. Einar, with his arm latched to his sister's tried to move gracefully across the stage, just as he had been taught. His actions continued until his sister was no longer moving gracefully with him. Although he did not hear Gertrude tell them to stop, Einar wanted to avoid any pain to his sister, so he ended the movements, which halted the practice.

Fortunately, even Gertrude was watching the disaster pace forward. The person approached nearer the stage. It stepped forward, left foot, stumble, right foot, stumble, to view Gertrude's masterpiece in the making a bit more closely. After capturing the attention of all the living figures in the theater, the person's face and figure were fully revealed to the entire cast. It was Aunt Evelyn. A sheer look of surprise, and perhaps a bit of angst, spread across the stage. As soon as the shock transposed onto the twins' faces, the aunt's image was lost in the stream of light that beckoned her forward. The twins felt momentary relief.

Any visit from the aunt was unexpected, considering her lack of attention and appreciation for the twins any time prior to that moment. But, her shocking visit would not have been so disconcerting if Einar knew that the aunt had accepted the verbal invitation from Gertrude during the previous Sunday's mass. Amazingly, the aunt's feeble attempt to be one of the "lord's creatures" was her only saving grace in the eyes of the agnostic male twin. It was the only sort of humanity she made visible. Unbeknownst to Einar, Aunt Evelyn actually had never attempted to be one of the lord's creatures; she was lured by the inexpensive edibles and liquids. Consequently, Aunt Evelyn had never skipped church. This was only because of its free servings of bread and wine. It was after her sixth shot of the Lord's blood that she verbally agreed to visit the theater. The devastating words of Kluge had haunted her. And in her thoughts, being a mother to "those creatures" would have hindered her lifestyle. Evelyn was adamant about her role, or the lack thereof, in the twins' lives, even if she almost entirely forgot about her acceptance to visit the theater in hopes to encourage the twins to continue working. Coincidentally, after the woman's daily morning bottle of Baldric's cheapest gas station Merlot, the subtle taste of the grape flavored vino reminded her of her promise. As she approached the stage, the morning dew had snuck up on the aunt, and her shuffle halted. Again, she vanished in the light.

"Am I dreaming?" Trixie asked. She was confused by the disappearing magical act.

Evelyn stood in the light, positioned just so, and remained a ghostly, unlike her usual ghastly, outline of a being.

"No Trix, a nightmare. You are experiencing a nightmare. As am I."

Gertrude interrupted the brief conversation between the twins. They were there to work. "Keep moving. That's it. Keep going; turn, turn, turn. Einar, raise your arms, higher, higher, higher." Gertrude increased his demands to show off all of the hard work that he was capable of manipulating from the twins and the puppets.

During the spectacle, Aunt Evelyn eventually found her way back into the visual path of the twins, and they watched her stride to the center seat in the front row and flop down into the flush material. Before the second act commenced, Gertrude instructed the entertainers to "Take cinco". Einar and even Trixie were quite learned in the basics of the Mexican tongue, so they understood his exact demand, as did everyone else on stage, who, with utmost precision, found their way to the wooden floor for a moment's rest.

"Braaaavvvvvo, braaaavvvvvo." The aunt vigorously clapped her hands to show her approval. Approval for what, she actually didn't know.

"What is *she* doing here?" Trixie questioned. It was a common question that Trixie often asked Einar shortly after spotting her mother's sister. The question was delayed only because Trixie did not understand why the aunt kept disappearing and then reappearing.

Unsure as to how to answer the question, Einar just moved forward and shrugged his shoulders. Trixie moved with him; her gaze was now fixed upon the woman who shared their surname.

With all of the actors at ease, Gertrude approached the woman. He began what looked to be a deep conversation with the aunt. Although it should have been private dialogue between the two adults, it was not. Gertrude stood just far enough away to deter the spread of alcohol through proximity and to avoid the tainted breath of the woman. Evelyn spoke much louder than necessary because of Gertrude's positioning, and the monkey, positioned much closer, overheard everything. Unfortunately, the twins did not hear everything. Einar leaned into the exchange, yet he was unable to decipher the entire discussion. He swayed forward to listen and heard snippets of the dialogue, of which he could not translate for his sister because of the murmurs of voices that interrupted the translation as he moved back.

Meanwhile, the monkey, restless from the lack of attention and annoyed by the boring conversation, opted to disengage the guest's focus upon Gertrude and began jumping around at the feet of Aunt Evelyn. When that failed, the animal dove for the lustrous canister that the woman attached to her hip. Once the flask was released from its compartment, the monkey marooned through the empty aisles and avoided any devastating halts to his mission.

By the time Aunt Evelyn realized her liquor was gone, she immediately interrupted the conversation with Gertrude and hysterically searched for the thief. "My syrup…oh, my syrup… it has been taken!" This probably could have been Evelyn's worst nightmare. It was utter chaos and quite a spectacle for the onlookers, namely the twins, until the inebriated aunt found the monkey sipping the bourbon in the corner. She tiptoed toward and cornered the swindler. "Give…that…back!" Evelyn shouted. She kept ordering commands at the monkey, as if it could understand what she was slurring. For the woman's sake, the animal's approaching drunkenness that reverberated through its paws allowed for the flask to easily slip into the hands of the rightful owner.

Gertrude, surfeited with the aunt's unnecessary frenzy, put the dolls and the twins back to work. It was not the work upon the stage that cued the aunt to leave; after the entire ordeal, her amnesia of why she was there in the first place took over and compelled her beyond the barrier of the theater, back into her own oblivion, with, of course, her flask in hand. She did not speak one single word to the twins.

The monkey fell asleep in the corner. It made no attempt to interrupt the rest of the rehearsal that had been as tedious and detrimental to the twins' physical beings as it had any day prior. After a multitude (and several half hours) of dizzying attempts of spins and jumps, the thespians were ordered to "Take cinco." Because of their hard work and the exasperating visit from the meddling aunt, the twins sat on the stage with the other dummies and disengaged their memories of the aunt from any recent, well, memory.

After their final "cinco," rehearsal ran well into the afternoon but ended near nightfall. The entire staff of the theater had quite a fulfilling day. Certainly, it was an appropriate time for Gertrude to slip a white envelope bulging with bills into Trixie's hand. It was also appropriate that Gertrude fully avoided the appropriations of the taxing system so that the business of theater and the arts operated under the most advantageous of situations. Gertrude had filled the envelope with two five dollar bills and twenty ones. Money was scarce in Baldric, large bills even more so.

Einar grabbed the envelope from his sister's hands and opened it as cautiously as he did with the mysterious envelope that appeared on his doorstep nearly a week prior. Again, because of Einar's lack of envelope opening experience, Einar's finger was fated with the same injury as before. The paper cut slice the top layers of his skin, and blood began to seep through the wound, but it was excitement, not curiosity, that led to his hastiness and the eventual injury. Fortunately, as he scooped the pile of bills out of the envelope and handed the wad to Trixie, personal bloodshed, oddly enough, did not plague the bills as it had the letter. "Count this," he necessitated. He wanted Trixie to feel accomplished, important. It was his paternal side rearing its head.

Trixie pretended to be a counting expert. She had seen the counting thing done before. She stopped and held out her fingers, which coincided with her counting. After counting twenty-five fingers while the wad lay on her lap, she finally spoke with much excitement. "Twenty-two. I counted twenty-two papers." Trixie, obviously unable to count money, had a distinguished opinion of the less than ample stash she held onto so tightly with her overwhelmed appendage that had been accustomed to making jazz hands for the director. She was also incorrect in her counting.

Einar realized that the girl could not have been correct about the amount of money that they had earned. He grabbed the stack of cash from her and began counting. To educate his sister of the economic world, he counted out loud, starting with the largest of the bills. "Trix, immerse your attention in how I calculate," he instructed. Then, Einar held up the two fives. "See the five? That symbolizes five." He stretched his fingers and raised his hand. He pushed one hand forward in front of the girl's face. "Five." He pushed the other hand in front of the girl's face. "Ten." This unnerving process continued with the ones, all twenty of them.

"How many dollars have I determined that we have earned?" This was one of the few times that Einar took time out of his personal agenda to encourage Trixie to be more knowledgeable. He figured that, at some point, she would need to know how to count and employ American currency, not the Baldric kind of currency.

Trixie was unaware that what she had just witnessed was a learning experience. She shrugged her shoulders at Einar's inquisition. Trixie's nonverbal signal did not perturb Einar, as he had fully realized the insufficiency of funds that he was holding in his hand. Einar called upon the man who suddenly vanished from their sights. "Gertrude...Gertrude," he hollered.

He called again, this time adding, Mzzz., senor, and senorita to the forefront of Gertrude's name, even if the Spanish words lacked any intended schwa. Then, Einar opted to move himself and Trixie off of the stage to settle at the table positioned in front of the rows of seats. As they stepped down the stage stairs, Einar did his best to scan the entire room. The sights before him were invaded by a dark emptiness. Neither Gertrude nor any of the puppets were noticeable or audible. And, Einar's exhaustion was too much to warrant a search party. So, he continued calling, "Ms. Gertrude, we have a question." He waited a few moments for a reply and when all was naught, he called again, "Mzzz. Gertrude? Senor Gertrude? Senorita Gertrude?"

From past the curtain and behind the stage, Einar finally heard a response. "Keep it down out there. You are bothering my peace and quiet. Can't a man relax?"

Not even recognizing that the voice established itself as a man, Einar was insistent in communicating with the person who he thought was Gertrude. "But, Gertrude, I am inquisitive about a particular matter."

Suddenly, the blue velour curtain that separated the backstage from the fore-stage split. The figure that approached from the waving sea of cloth exhibited the miniature human that had also previously measured the twins' bodies. "Do I look like Gertrude?" He asked. The midget's masculinity doubled that of Gertrude's as he stood on the stage in front of the gush of fabric. He had waited for the moment when he could confront the twins. They had a detrimental impact on the life that the midget was used to living. He spoke of this. "Well, well, the usurpers of my glorious, idolized career. Now, I am a measly behind-the-scenes worker. You have stripped me of my life, my happiness. All in the name of theater."

"Which one are you?" Trixie asked. She ignored the midget's displeasure with her and her sibling. She wanted to know which one of the puppets he was because she suddenly believed that the puppets did have a breath of life. Trixie had forgotten that she had already met the guy. Of course, to her benefit, the newsboy cap did make him look different, and this day, his head was uncovered. The air whisked through his thin, graying hair.

"I am Morton, madam." Morton's tawdry confidence exuded

as he answered. "You, my dears," Morton now looked more closely at the twins. He squinted his eyes to ensure that what was positioned before him was not a mirage. He continued, "are phenoms."

Not understanding the fascination the midget had with them, Einar diverted the conversation to something more meaningful than his own eccentric being, his wages. "Is it normal to be paid so little?" Not meaning to ostracize the man, Einar reiterated his question. "Is it normal to have such inadequate earnings?" And again, before the midget could answer, Einar reiterated his message to avoid any diminutive references. "We have been paid a deficient amount of earnings. Is this customary?"

"Paid? You earn pay? Well, well, isn't that interesting?" Confused, Morton neared the table. He stood at the edge, leaned over, and scratched his head and twirled his graying locks with an adventurous finger.

"You mean you do not earn pay?" Einar was as interested in Morton's fiscal plan as he was his own.

"Let's just say that I don't pay for any amenities while I travel, and since I don't do anything except wander this grand earth, well, I don't need any earnings. Aren't you earning lodging and, for goodness sakes, food?" Morton, taking a sudden liking for the twins, really regretted the last comment. He knew full well, because of Einar's robust stature, that the twins did not go without proper nutrition.

"We have lodging and food, but upkeep, that is my concern."

Morton took a few moments to realize that he was being taken for granted. As his fingers tapped along the edge of the table, Gertrude, burst through the side door and interrupted the meeting as best he knew how. He shouted, "What is the prob..." His observation interrupted his demand at first sight of the midget. "You!" He sniveled the remark. "What are you doing? Go back," he shouted. Then, he pointed toward the curtain that moved to fully reveal the workspace but meant back far beyond it. "If you know what is good for you." The final remark was a threat.

"Yeah, I know what is good for me." Morton postured as statuesque as his height could afford. He then placed his hands on his hips, nearly copying the man in the dress. He continued his tease, "A few dollars, some yen, if you can afford, and maybe even some francs; that's what's good for me."

"Go! Vamos!" Gertrude instructed, again.

"No! No!" Morton refused, again.

"You'll not take money from these hard working civili, um, things." Gertrude meant to say civilians, but found that 'things' was more descriptive term for the twins.

Einar tried to protrude into the fiasco. "But we…"

"You, nothing. Get up on that stage. And you, little one, if you want to have a name for yourself in this town or any other, you do as I say." Gertrude spoke with more breadth and severity than ever, and all who were in that vacant room that day heard an echo resounding the demand that made even the light shades shiver.

The twins and the midget, facing the tirade and fearing the worst, did as instructed and returned to the stage and beyond for more rigorous practice.

"You dispute; we work more. Mas, mas, mas," Gertrude dictated.

And that they did. They worked more, more, more, as Gertrude so delicately ordered. He certainly held true to his statement. For the rest of the evening, the twins were forced to continue their twists and turns and their leaps and jumps, and Morton was forced to continue to do whatever he did behind the curtain.

Nearing midnight, as the moon infiltrated the sky, Gertrude decisively liberated the workers. He granted them an "adios" in a not so friendly farewell tone. Einar and Trixie scurried to gather their belongings and escape the location and the sounds of the scattered Spanish demands. They stepped back onto the concrete that led them to that dismal place. With every prod and trod, they paced closer and closer to the enclosed Plexiglas structure that marked the edge of the territory of the theater. They only slowed their pace once.

"Trix, is something audible?"

"Huh?" She responded. The poor girl could barely keep her eyes open, let alone her ears.

"Never mind." Einar could barely attempt a conversation, let alone one with his sister.

They continued the path, nearing the portal of sanity, the rectangular glass bus stop enclosure that was opportune for hiding the effects of natural forces. Trixie, in charge of the change because it made a clingity, clankity melody in her pocket as she walked, fumbled to find the four magical quarters that could lead them to the heavenly bliss of their home. Gertrude and the theater had suddenly replaced the abhorring images and feelings that Einar had of Lola. Home was going to be quite a welcoming place.

Within only a few minutes, enough time for Einar to realize his appreciation of home, the moving carriage arrived. The twins trampled up the stairs, and Trixie filled the metal slot with the allotted coins necessary for their travels. Just as soon as the change hit the bottom of the change box and the bus started rolling away, the driver eased the vehicle to a halt. They were going nowhere quickly; it was ironic.

"What? Why the delay?" Einar shouted. He did not want nowhere to be his destination.

"Um miss, sir, you owe two quarters." The driver spoke quietly.

Trixie turned around to face the driver's face in the mirror. The gentle eyes peering into the mirror cajoled the girl for a hurried response.

"Sir, I counted," she paused to count to four on her fingers and continued, "this many." She held up her four childish counting fingers, which were obviously getting much use. She then reaffirmed, "And I heard four clanks."

Einar interjected, "Do we owe more?" It wasn't the question that should have encouraged the man's response; it was the sudden glance of Einar's eyes over the bodies that he and his twin inhabited.

"No sir, but," and the driver ever so graciously looked not toward the twins but down toward the rubber runner seeped with remnants of daily travel.

Trixie's eyes trailed those of the driver. And she noticed, as did Einar, that Morton was curiously standing behind the both of them.

Einar, enraged at the escapee of the theater, yelled too loudly for an unoccupied bus, "Go pay the man, Morton."

Morton, almost mocking the severity of Einar's voice, showed his empty pockets and replied, "Got no cash." He fidgeted his fingers in the pockets and restated his previous remark. "Nope. I have nothing." At least Morton was honest. He did not have anything except the clothes on his back and whatever fit into his handy backpack.

"Of course, and where do you expect to travel with no cash?" Einar asked.

"To some nice, cozy home in this town. Know of any?"

Morton looked at Trixie and then poked her. The girl, bolstered by the coercing jab of the midget, glanced toward her brother and pleaded, "We have a nice, cozy home. Can we keep him? Pleeaaassseee?"

The driver interrupted this bizarre exchange. "Um, guys, I need two quarters. You're not the only ones wanting to go home."

Einar, who always kept extraneous quarters, tossed the

revered coins to the midget castaway. "Give the man his quarters."

Morton's response was sincere, "Gracias." And after the proper thanking, Morton marched up to the driver with as much pomp and circumstance that a midget could afford and gave the nice man the change.

NINE

The Night will Obscurely Unfold

After the scandalous day, the intermittent family- the two twins and one intrusive midget- exited the bus and slowly paced along the winding pathway, through the thickets, and into the warm home that likened a cozy shack outfitted with attached, once outdoor, facilities. With everyone was safely inside, Einar stuck his head out of the door to ensure that there were no secret invites or visitors lying within the realm of his eyesight. When the coast was clear, he closed the door and locked it. After realizing that his and Trixie's exhaustion was, in part, caused by their lack of nourishment, Einar scoured the fridge for any food to feed Trixie, himself, and the small man.

"So, little man, what is your agenda here?" Einar leaned fully into the appliance situated in the corner of the kitchen as he questioned the visitor. Trixie leaned with him, although she had less of an interest in finding edibles in the fridge.

Morton answered, "I want to talk business; you know, money, advancement, opportunities. There must be all three for all of us, somewhere. You know clone?" Morton had years of criticism, and he compelled the need to share his ceaseless anger.

Trixie, still enthralled by her new houseguest which she likened to "the pet I never had", just watched the two men banter.

"Well, what are you thinking?" Einar, perhaps due to his sudden awareness of his own disability, began to listen to Morton.

Before Morton could speak, Trixie interrupted, "I want some

cottage cheese." She had finally found disinterest in the conversation and the guest and found interest in the food stock stored in the appliance. Cottage cheese was a staple, inexpensive, non-government issued food that was a cheap luxury for the members of Baldric, thanks to the local dairy farm. Few households did without the local delicacy.

"Not now Trix," Einar responded, although he entirely ignored her question.

"And some frozen vegetables. Can we cook those?" Trixie asked as she hovered over her brother and reached as far as she could into the freezer. She then pointed at the packaged vegetables.

Einar, knowing the likelihood that his sister would persistently interrupt any intelligent conversations the men would think about having, decided to decide upon dinner before anything else transpired. "Yes, Trix, we can have the cottage cheese and vegetables." He then quickly put Trixie to work, like most men did to women. Einar did, of course, help, since he knew that Trixie could somehow find a way to ruin dinner.

Like most of the things that the twins did, the preparation of dinner was tedious. They worked in the insufficiently spaced kitchen-turned-canteen due to the addition of the uninvited foreigner. Morton aided the twins by avoiding the bustle and investigating his surroundings. He visualized spiders seducing their prey in the intricate webs that hung along the wooden laths lining the ceiling. The imposter florals were precisely arranged within a myriad of vases situated around the room. They added domesticity to the otherwise dismal aura of the residence.

While attempting to decipher the scarce capacity between the four walls, Morton soon scanned the olive green carpeting that oozed like a disease throughout the house. The assortment of stains and burns added a peculiar character to the covering.

A brief clatter of the pan hitting the metal sink aroused

Morton's reality. This reality was becoming clearer. Images of the shabby home and the shabby town because of the brief bus ride that toured the shambles of Baldric shot through Morton's memory. Plus, the paper plates and plastic dining furniture alerted him of the Smith twins' situation. Although never earning pay, Morton lived a life of luxury. The life that he had just chosen to enter was not luxurious. He momentarily began to sympathize with the twins just when the rustle of the plating interrupted his thoughts. Any other emotion also disappeared the moment he heard the fine words spoken by both twins in unison after they had successfully outfitted the dining area with plates of food, glasses of milk, and a votive of lit, homemade candles, "Dinner's ready!" Trixie exclaimed.

After not eating for hours, they were all starving. Everyone rushed to find appropriate seating and began devouring the food. Situated at the dinner table that was decorated with paper plates, makeshift paper towel placemats, and waxy ambiance set ablaze, Morton voraciously chowed the elaborate dinner of fully thawed peas and cottage cheese. He adjoined both foods into one large pile on his plate. His plate likened those of the twins as they all mashed and mixed the meal together. The muted midget, who incessantly shoveled his food into his largely dis-proportioned mouth, and the lack of pandemonium from the kitchen created an odd quietness among the trio. It endured nearly the entirety of the meal until Morton uttered, "Mmm...this is good." As he spoke, Morton reached for a napkin across the table. His reduced sized and his inability to chew and reach caused him to falter and lose balance. He attempted to grasp onto anything on the table to keep him from falling off of the bench. When he settled, one fatal swoop of his arm swept across the glass of milk that was nesting close to his body. He regained his balance, but the milk lost its own and trickled off of the vinyl, yellow gingham tablecloth. The liquid spread across the table, soaked into the paper set-up, and dripped onto the sickly looking carpet. Morton struggled to contain the accident, but his arms would not give in to his mind that wanted them to reach just the slightest bit further. All he could do was create a barrier at the edge of the table. This he did quite effectively with his stubs.

Trixie's first reaction was to rush into the kitchen to attain the large tattered sponge her late mother used to soak up any devastating spills caused by the twins. She attempted to pull away from her brother's restraint, but he, quickly assembling the place mats to clean the mess, did not budge from his seat. Einar's swift movements and cautionary control saved the flooring from another fatal marking. Morton was simply embarrassed. "My apologies," he said, as the twins continued to clean. They nodded in acceptance and finished cleaning the spilled milk.

Because of the accident, the dinner rested upon soaked paper platters. It was clear that the dining experience was over. Everyone was nearly finished anyhow, so the pre-dinner, doleful atmosphere returned. Soon, conversational sounds invaded the dwelling as the inhabitants and the guest moved two steps into the petite living space. The trio settled onto the tattered couch centered along the back wall where a picture still maintained the livelihood of Lola. If only the monkey was there, he could have drawn Morton into the ensemble.

Forgetting about the sympathetic moment that he had experienced before eating, Morton became increasingly jealous of the monetary transaction between Gertrude, a man who served as Morton's maternal influence, and Einar and Trixie. Morton too wanted to slather his fingers with a pile of endless, crisp bills. The jealously, though, did not replace the increasing gratitude that he had for the twins, especially Einar, who always seemed to have everything under control. Morton also realized that his newfound relationship with the twins allowed for him to experience freedom, freedom away from his menacing boss. Morton was not once regretting his escape, and he, clearly, was not ready to relinquish his freedom. Plus, he really enjoyed the Baldric cottage cheese. He just wanted some money.

Situated on the couch, his feet firmly pressing against the stale air, Morton spoke, "Riddle me this. What would Gertrude and his amazing show do without you and me? Better yet, what would he do without us *and* the marionette dolls?"

"Why yes, he would be disoriented without his pawns." Einar found the comment of Morton to be quite keen. "So, master of plans, what do you suggest we arrange? Shall we organize a heist? Shall we renounce our positions?" Einar asked. He implied some spectacular schemes held in by the silence of dinner.

Yet, Morton had something else in mind about which he spoke so fervently. "A strike. I propose a strike." Morton's jealously was not quite visible. Perhaps it was fleeting.

In congruence to Morton's plan, Einar raised his glass of ice-cold milk to his counterpart's more empty glass and verbally agreed. "Yes, that is it, a strike! Genius, my friend."

The clink of the glasses was commencement enough for their ingenious plan until Einar quizzically asked, "What is a strike?" Innocently aware and unaware of much, Einar could attribute his knowledge and the lack thereof from the books offered to him by his mother. Lola bought most of the out of date, out of print, or censored books at the annual library sale; none of Einar's books ever once contained mention of a strike. Einar's personal moments of genius was oft halted by a missing link of information.

"Really?" Morton questioned. He was suddenly aware that his hasty move to befriend the twins might not be as fruitful as once determined, even if they could prepare a substantial meal. "A strike is when workers refuse to work based on unfair conditions. We, my friend, work under unfair conditions and should organize a strike." Thankfully for Einar, Morton was like a walking pamphlet of his own and offered information that Einar did not know existed. Morton had suddenly filled a void and became Einar's missing link.

"Well, what will come of it?" Einar asked as he slowly began to understand the idea of a strike and then began to explore the option and its benefits.

"Gertrude could give us more pay. He could improve our working conditions, give us more time for lunch, treat us better. We want shorter work days. We want more delicate orders. We want to work in a kinder, gentler environment..." Morton continued with his explanation atop his soapbox for several minutes while Einar fervently listened. Trixie just laid her head on the shoulder of the couch. Her eyelids wavered above her eyes while she listened to the background strums of the men's voices. Eventually, the shutters of her eyes fully closed and the voices faded. Theater work, or any work at all, was difficult for the twin.

Alert and anxious, Einar carefully observed Morton's words. He, fully cognizant that there was always a duplicate side to everything, suddenly realized that a strike might not end in their benefit. "What if Gertrude chooses not to give us our demands?"

"We quit." Morton acted as if that was an obvious idea. "Simple problems have simple solutions," he added.

"Quit the strike? Then what is the purpose?" Einar was perplexed.

Shaking his head, Morton attempted to absolve any of Einar's confusion. "We will not quit the strike; we will quit the theater. Gertrude can do nothing without us. The show cannot go on." Morton sat back and stared down at his miniature body, and then he stared at the clones.

Einar finally understood what Morton was trying to establish for the second time. They were, all three of them, unique. It was an aspect of their lives that Einar was slowly realizing. Gertrude not succumbing to the needs of the workers would be considerably preposterous on his part.

After thoughtful consideration, the two men situated next to the sleeping girl, drew their plans for the impending strike, and then they drew their signs for the same endeavor. Morton, secretly ambidextrous, just as Einar could have been if he was not hunched over his sister sleeping upright, quickly amassed quite a variety of signs and posters that would work well for the strike that the men planned for the next day. At the end of the night after Einar quaffed the rest of his celebratory milk, the theater thespians laid three in a row. They slept off the day's work and the fulfilling peas and cheese. Their hearts and minds, at least those of the men, awaited the rising sun to meet with their futures.

TEN

A Worker's Fake Paradise

Early in the morning, the twins, along with their newly acquired midget, anxiously trampled through the brushes and thickets and down the weeded cement that led them to the bus stop. This time, Morton was not hiding behind the twins when they stepped onto the mode of transportation. He was front and center and proud of his epiphany and the cohorts that followed his lead. The bus ride mimicked their week—a mindless, doldrum affair. But this time, even if it was the morning, Einar felt a sense of exuberance. It was nice for a change.

The trio arrived at their destination, where their destiny would be determined that day. They exited the conclaves of the vehicle and the wind swept through their array of posters that were colored with the brightest hues of the primary colors. Trixie's was splattered with silver glitter. The men did this in hopes of distracting the girl from the reality of their intentions. Neither had time to actually explain the details of the strike to Trixie, and their plan worked as they stood outside of the theater and motioned for her to follow. She did, and as she followed, she glanced at the shimmering cardboard every so often. Trixie's fascination of the bright shimmers caused her to move past the stopped men. Her sight was affixed on the shining sun that reflected off of the metal door until the force of Einar's arm halted her away from the entrance that was just within reach.

"We will not enter today." Einar's intense articulation

surprised Trixie. She knew better than to respond.

Morton began a circular march and enticed the twins to follow the pattern. With no choice but to walk together with the men, Trixie soon yielded to their physical fortitude. "Follow me," Morton encouraged. And with that, all three workers promenaded in a circular fashion and shouted the types of poignant remarks that most striking workers would shout. The morning onlookers, namely the few people on the bus that passed the theater every fifteen minutes and the few otherwise miserable participants in Baldric's workforce who jaunted to work on foot each morning, passed and stared, but none stopped. The one sole observer, the monkey, did nothing but sit in the doorway, scratch his nether regions, and feel the waft of the wind whisk though his fur. The strike did little to catch the monkey's attention.

"Where are they?" Morton inquired about the observers that he assumed would watch his spectacle. He was obviously impatient.

Einar questioned, "They who?" He was not attune to Morton's assumptions, and he certainly didn't know that there were supposed to be other participants.

"The spectators," Morton responded. Being in the entertainment industry for so long, Morton always expected the utmost attention. Ultimately, he was certain that an impressive strike would have to include a myriad of crowds that assembled because of their proposition. He never thought that their proposition could be meaningless to everyone else. Of course, he was also slightly narcissistic.

As the buses and pedestrians passed, the crowd, as Morton anticipated, did not form. Not feeling an immediate, or even eventual, effect of their dominant scheme, he decided to move the mutiny into the theater where at least one person, Gertrude, would notice. He prompted his fellow strikers to march into the dark complex of the theater. The twins heeded to his prompting and cautiously slipped through the opening of the door.

Inside by the ticket window, the cross-dressing hermaphrodite was busy placing the enlarged caricatures of the stars of his show inside the even larger frames. The entrance, lit by the glowing rays of sunlight emulated the posters of more successful thespians from the years past, when the theater was entertainment, and business kept its distance. Times had changed drastically.

Trixie followed her fellow strikers, and her sight projected toward the drawings prepared by none other than the mischievous monkey. The portraits showed her face glowing with sweat while her head was positioned upon her brother's shoulder. The elevated paintings showed their tiring struggle as entertainers, as beings, and as people with only a small piece of frame separating their identities.

"You're late." Gertrude neither noticed the mutinous midget nor the signs of ambiguously literal protest.

Morton prominently stepped nearer the director and attempted to obstruct Trixie's view from her own drawn portrait. She continued her gaze, never once noticing the midget marching forward.

Morton spoke, "No, we aren't late. We demand shorter work days." The midget was stern and decided to begin his particular rants with one of the most realistic demands.

"Nothing about you needs to get any shorter. Prepare for work." Gertrude iterated his opinion of the midget's height and the length of the work day.

Avoiding any emotion from the hurtful response, Morton tried to negotiate another aspect of their work. "We need more pay."

"You're paid enough. Prepare for work. Ahora," Gertrude responded.

"Ms. Gertrude," Einar now tried his attempt to convince the chieftain, "we cannot live upon thirty dollars per week. It is unjust, unfair, and simply intolerable."

Reiterating his point again, Gertrude repeated, "You're paid fairly. Get to work." He paused, took a deep, long breath, and shouted, "AHORA."

With no other theater jobs to juxtapose earnings, the trio was almost convinced that they might have acted in jest. Perhaps in comparison to other wages of other jobs, they were paid fairly. Einar and Morton considered this, yet Trixie, actively pursued her actions from the exterior of the theater. "We won't work until we're paid enough." The sight of her own face plastered upon the wall strengthened her convictions as a striking worker, and money, as if it defined her success, had become mutually important. At least, that was what she recalled from her short-term memory of her outside endeavors; the glimmering sign and interminable shouting proved this for the female, although she actually would not know what to do with any hard earned cash, except donate it to the shiny box of the Transportation Authority.

Annoyed by the twins and the devious midget, Gertrude just stomped away and left the strikers at a standstill. The faint breeze, caused by Gertrude dramatically passing the strikers, infiltrated the air nearest the box office and tousled the golden strands of the twins' hair.

"What should we do now?" Einar questioned. He was miffed that his plans never seemingly worked out as planned. He worried about his position in the theater and his position as a striking worker just as the slight burst of wind caused a chill. He felt Lola's presence, not realizing the true cause of the draft.

Morton assured the twin. "We will continue." Morton was convinced that they would get their own way. Also chilled, he only recognized the draft that swelled from the passing of the oversized drama queen, not the draft from the passing of Lola.

"Are there any more?" Trixie asked. She was also becoming a necessary attachment to the plan.

"More what?" Morton questioned.

Before Trixie could answer, Einar interjected. "More strikers, more force."

His interruption came right before Trixie would verbally wonder if there was going to be more marching and shouting.

By this time, Morton caught on to Einar's assertion. "Ahhh yes, the marionettes. They're what we need."

Morton, impressing the most agile of thieves with his criminal like stance, stood on his toes and surveyed his surroundings. Without notice or warning, he bolted through the lobby and ran toward the stage. He stopped only once to examine the area again. The twins nonchalantly followed and waited as Morton snuck into the back of the stage and dragged the dolls out one by one. He then quickly released the dolls into the hands of the twins. When his mission was finished, Morton, weighted with two of the puppets hanging at his side, stealthily snuck back into the front side of the theater, and the twins, wrestling with the four others, careened after him.

With the dolls situated and aligned outside of the cement square, the twins and midget initiated their shenanigans once again. Within a few moments, as the eleventh hour of the day approached, the strikers, finally, received the attention they wanted. Passersby and onlookers suddenly became rubberneckers and crowds. Word passed slowly through the town, and by the time it reached the furthest place of business, Sally's Hair Emporium, all the loquacious listeners, flipping through magazines as their hearing was muffled by the sound of the hot air swirling their scalps, heard nothing short of spiked punch at Peter's, the home of the local AA host. Regardless of the intended message, "a striking bunch outside the theater", the town was in an uproar. As Aunt Evelyn and a handful of other parched souls headed to Peter's for the afternoon, the others surrounded the metal gate encasing the theater.

Baldric's infamously fabulous news reporter slash well-endowed stripper, Melanie Jefferson, also caught wind of an upheaval at the theater. Melanie had a nose for the news, and she was certainly Baldric's most glorified female, being a public figure and all. She stepped out of her van and was followed by the cameraman. With microphone in hand, she stepped off of the sidewalk and through the gates. Her approach toward the display titillated the midget.

"Why hello there," Morton greeted. He used his most distinguished gentleman voice, although he lacked the essence of a genteel being. Suddenly, he lacked focus for their endeavor outlined so brilliantly the night before.

The heiress to Baldric's most fortunate family's wealth was poised in her professional stance, the one as a news reporter. She ignored the greeting and aimed her concentration into the camera that followed her entrance onto the theater lawn. "This is Melanie Jefferson coming to you from outside of the theater, where two, or maybe three, people have staged some sort of riot." Melanie now turned her attention to the twins. "What is the purpose of this riot?" she asked.

"Riot," Einar explained, "You must be mistaken. This is a strike. Riot? We would not think to do such a thing." Ms. Jefferson rolled her eyes at the male who could have answered her question with a simple "No". The camera zoomed away from Einar's face and centered upon both twins after the male twin spoke to the people of Baldric. Soon enough though, just as Trixie was ready to shout remarks similar to those that she had shouted all morning, the cameraman diverted his device and scanned the entire scene that was comprised of four marionettes, a monkey dragging two of the dolls away from the sight, a pair of twins, and a midget. It was a normal day for the news.

Vying for any attention, Morton, after stealing a top hat and pliable machete off of a fully costumed wooden doll, raced toward the camera and the beauty. "On guard!" he spluttered while trying to show off his playful side.

Catching the woman off guard, Morton became increasingly enamored with the media host donned in her finest business attire and fashionable five-inch clear stilettos as she stumbled to catch the microphone that popped out of her hands upon sight of his frightening display. She thought he was anything but playful.

Composing her demeanor, the reporter turned to the camera again. She continued to ignore the incessant attempts from the midget. "Well folks, it is a strike, or perhaps, just some freak show maneuver to advertise the dwindling art of the theater." Melanie would have continued her investigation, but her explanation was interrupted by the soft voice in her ear. She addressed the audience, "I am hearing word about another revolt across town. For now, this is Melanie Jefferson; we will return briefly with another thorough inquiry into this second riot. Good day Baldric." The woman turned from the camera and began walking toward the entrance.

Morton, shouting, "It's not a riot; it's a strike," followed Ms. Jefferson until she disappeared into the fortuitous media's white van that sped off. The vanishing vehicle left the midget distressed and silly looking in the doll's attire. Einar and Trixie watched as the midget, with his head hung low, stomped through the also dissipating crowds.

After posing for the camera, the monkey, coping with the boredom creeping in, continued to drag the puppets one by one back into the theater. The camera caught the misanthrope wielding the dolls, but his capture did not deter him; he was determined to return the puppets to their necessary posts and then close the door on the disorderly scene that he witnessed.

Receptive to his master's intentions, the monkey found leverage upon a metal stool situated nearest the door; he then locked the entrance in hopes of keeping the riotous bunch from entering. Inside, Gertrude waited for his monkey to return and then coerced the intelligent species into the theater van. The perverse diversion from the media and the crowds allowed Gertrude to take his monkey and flee the scene. As the troupe marched around, the screeching tires and Gertrude yelling, "Adios" out of the van window as he sped down the street should have been clues to the twins and the midget that Gertrude and his monkey were not returning. The strikers actually did not notice, and Gertrude was free to eventually settle miles away from the menacing workers and much nearer a relaxing body of water. Mexico, with its cheap beer and even cheaper labor, was the chosen destination. Clearly, he did not mind if anyone located him. And, although he had a great passion for the American theater, Gertrude feared a worker's strike would hinder his success and burden his bank account.

As the director drove further away, the three strikers continued with their cause. When Trixie tired, the men agreed to enter the theater and sit in the cozy chairs, just as the girl wanted. Since they were unaware of the escape, the locked front door was quite a shock. "That conniving, asshole!" Morton exclaimed as he reached the door handle and shook it fiercely to no avail. The theater door was not going to open.

"Maybe he forgot to unlock it?" Trixie, a bit perplexed by their inability to enter their place of employment, spoke about the monkey that she watched jiggle the handle in an effort to amuse itself.

"Is there a hind door to this structure?" Einar asked. He was befuddled by the event that was unfolding that day, became increasingly concerned about his position in the workforce that he so strongly fought against for a mere four hours.

Trixie was confused by Einar's questioning. All she knew was that they were obviously standing in front of a door, hind or not.

Ultimately, the investigation led the troupe slowly to the back of the theater where they eventually found the unlocked opening of the theater. It was the most favorable endeavor of the day for the unemployed trio, even if they did not know that they were abandoned and jobless. They neared the posterior door when Morton began his derogatory blaspheme once again. "That evil, god damned prick." Morton knew the man better than he let on and suddenly realized the malfunction of their plan. Gertrude didn't really need any of them. His greed for money could be trumped by a major bothersome display, such as the one he witnessed earlier. And Morton suddenly realized the voice behind the "adios" and the meaning of the word. He led the trio de resistance to the door as the wind blew it from side to side. It mocked the vacancy of the once thriving place of entertainment. The sweat had dried, and all that was left were an assortment of idle dolls that were piled so kindly by the monkey in the corner of the stage. "We're done." They all lost their chances. To ensure that the twins understood, Morton explained, "He left. Gertrude and that obnoxious animal left."

Trixie repeated the observance, much like she repeated everything that Morton had said that day. "Gertrude left?"

The answer, given by both Einar and Morton, was simple and monotonous, "Yes."

They all entered the theater. It was their final entrance, and they knew it. The group's grief settled in. Motionless, they stood silent for moments until Trixie diverted her attention to the pile of marionettes. The dolls were desolate and alone, and Trixie was saddened by the sight. The wooden-faced strikers stared into the empty seats of the hollow playhouse. And the dolls stared too, although they stared at the ceiling where the light once shone upon their brilliantly Chinese-crafted carcasses.

"What do you suggest we do now maestro?" Einar growled at the short man. Before him, Einar did not even know what a strike was. He fully experienced how one could go awry, and he did not like the outcome of it.

"Well, you replica," Morton did not appreciate the growl. He explained, "We can obviously strike the attention of the peasant folk of Baldric."

"All these peasant folk you speak of obviously did us no good. Their attention, even that of the few non peasants of the persistent media, did not aid in our quest."

"But people should take a liking toward," Morton stopped and looked cautiously at Trixie and then at Einar, as if to make a more bold, egotistical statement yet continued, "us. I say we do something that can get people's attention, bigger this time."

"I have had enough of Baldric citizens and their attempt to give us attention. Nobody, not a single person, showed that they believed in our cause." Einar was angry that nobody aided them and the attention given them was trite.

"You don't like people looking at you Einar?" The midget's question was poignant and almost hurtful.

Einar's response was harsh, "No."

"I do," Trixie responded. From the moment she felt the eyes of the puppets and saw her own figure displayed in front of her from the lens of the camera and from the picture that derived out of the genius of the monkey, she momentarily liked the image.

"She does." Morton pointed toward the sister.

"She just does not have the capacity to understand." Einar didn't care whose feelings he hurt that day and made the especially harmful remark after years of tolerating Trixie's questioning of what felt like his every word. He was fully feeling the impact of rejection and strife and the dealings with, as he would label, "the uneducated and misguided". Nothing could have changed his mind. And, Einar suddenly realized that perhaps Lola, from the grave, single-handedly, indirectly influenced the events that unfolded that day.

In an effort to conclude all conversation, Einar wandered. He dragged his sister with him toward the paralyzed wooden figures. One by one, he picked up the dolls and handed them to Trixie. The dolls stared at his every move, but that time, that one time, Einar did not care about the glances. He knew they didn't have minds to judge him or his sister, especially since they never even looked down to view the funny looking small man.

ELEVEN

<u>The Hero is the King</u>

The trio, exhaustive of any other ingenious plan, headed home. They were unfortunate and desperate. As they walked, they hauled the wooden mutes down the sidewalk. Unable to spend any monetary units on excess, Einar thought it was more appropriate for them to bypass the luxury of public transportation. His plan of utilizing the less convenient mode of transportation while they all carried the weighty marionettes had come to fruition, only after a bit of a negotiation between the twins. Yet, with Einar's more masculine physique, Trixie had little say. And, after only a few minutes of walking, Trixie, regardless of her inexhaustible attempt to coerce Einar to ride that "big bus", forgot about her argument and was actually content to stroll through Baldric and look at the scenery, although most of the scenery was anything but pristine.

Ironically, the girl, who initially had been less than pleased with the feat of walking home, had become quite content and actually astute. "Loki Kluge!" It was one of the more less than pristine scenes she had spotted. She liked how the name sounded as she rolled it off of her tongue, so she said it again, more intensely, as she pointed across the street. "Lokiiii Klugggge."

Einar, wearied by the dolls he carried, finally caught wind of what Trixie was trying to establish, and that sparked an idea. He hurried along, trying to catch up with the man that Trixie saw across the street.

"Mr. Kluge, Mr. Kluge, we must speak with you," Einar's voice was hurried and breathless as he towed Trixie and Morton toward the lawyer who was standing on the sidewalk next to the vegetable cart. The lawyer was picking out the freshest of edibles at Baldric's shanty form of a farmer's market.

Kluge turned, melon in one hand and a revered cigarette slim 100 in the other. He took the slim and, in a celebratory fashion, dragged a hit, as if to denote another successful day at the Law Office of Kluge and Kluge. Kluge turned to fully face the three, a troupe of weirdoes holding a myriad of wooden dolls running at him with less than lightening speed. The scene startled him a bit, and he fumbled the melon, catching it between his breast and his elbow. It stayed there as he imagined bandits vying to usurp him of his last good puff and his beautifully round melon. Quickly, Kluge rolled the fruit back into his hand and grasped the cigarette tighter between his fingers and inhaled to take a final smoky breath before he threw the tobacco filled tube at the feet of the twins and midget who finally infiltrated his personal space. He just stood and waited for the proper hello. And, after assuming that the proper welcoming would not occur, he spat his tobacco-flavored saliva onto the sidewalk, as if he was waiting for a showdown.

"Mr..." Einar took a moment to catch up with his breathlessness, "Kluge...we must speak with you."

Kluge turned back around and said, "I'll take two."

This confused Trixie who held onto her dolls just a bit more tightly. Kluge, clearly was speaking to the vegetable cart connoisseur; he was not referencing the marionettes. He turned back around, purchase in hand. "Now?"

"Now is preferable, since we must speak to you about some urgent matters."

The urgent matters of which Einar spoke piqued Kluge's interest. He, of course, figured that the twins needed him to employ them, which was not their intention at all. "Well, if you have to talk to me now," Kluge paused and waited to see how urgent Einar thought his matters were.

"Yes, yes, now would be most suitable," Einar gushed.

"On my terms?" Kluge asked. He had become accustomed to having most things on his own terms, but he did like to throw out the question to make his counterparts feel equal to his mighty status.

"Whatever you would like Mr. Kluge." Surprisingly, Einar was quite cordial with the man who he had publicly detested on several occasions, but, of course, Einar did need Kluge's advice, so he wanted to be as kind as his need would warrant.

"Follow me," the lawyer instructed.

Morton was the first to heed to Kluge's directions. He quickly turned and began to follow until he stopped and turned to see the twins still standing. He asked, "Whatta ya waiting for?"

The twins, slightly exhausted from their walk from the theater, watched Morton turn back around and skip behind Kluge. They soon followed suit.

Kluge walked briskly through the streets of Baldric. He waited upon every street corner to stop and allow all of the followers to catch up to him. When the faction was within eyesight, Kluge ambled his way across the busy cross streets, only to wait on the other side. The monotonous trek of walking, stopping, turning, walking… would have been quite exasperating for Kluge, but every time he turned to look at the trio, he visualized dollar signs. The walk alone would earn Kluge something monetary, since he could not imagine the twins and the midget paying in any other form.

Once the group successfully ambled through the busy thoroughfare, Kluge waited once again. This time it was for everyone to catch up with him before he turned and walked toward Tolbett's Hill. The man's eyes fixated on the large warehouse. It was the only building at the foot of the hill, for obvious reasons. Earnest Tolbett had been a Baldric pioneer. Earnest Tolbett had also been Baldric's infamous serial killer. This hill was, oddly, named after him after Baldric's sheriff found a mountain of dead prostitutes at the bottom of the hill. Ironically, the whole dead prostitute episode led to Baldric's more effective law: No person or persons shall, under any circumstance, receive pay for sexual acts. This law, paired with the town's dire economic situation, prompted the people to realize that sex could be used for bartering, hence their current practices. Kluge was reminded of this historical nugget every time he walked to his family's warehouse at the foot of Tolbett's Hill. Since the tragic events were long past, Kluge had little emotion and continued his movement until he stopped at the door.

Although Einar was open to exploring the world, Kluge's location prompted him to feel a little less secure about his hopes and dreams and much less secure about scouring every inch of Baldric. "What is this place?" It was a rhetorical question as he certainly knew that Trixie would not have answered. His concern became so overwhelming that it led to a verbal regurgitation of sorts.

Trixie did hear her brother and just shrugged. Of course, if he did not know what that place was, she did not either.

Morton, whose pace had slowed up to the twins, insisted upon answering any question thrown his way. Verbal regurgitation was his forte. "It is, dear twin, a building, a very large building."

Einar ignored the obvious comment and kept inching forward. He was arm in arm with his sibling as Kluge waved his arms erratically, as if the twins could not recognize the only man standing at the bottom of the only hill that surrounded them.

When the twin's freckles were visible by Kluge's naked eye, he fumbled for his chain of keys. In due time, the appropriate key was placed into the appropriate key hole, and Kluge opened the door into a vast, gray emptiness. The building had been hollowed out, and the only things visible were a table and chairs that centered in the vacant space and piles of large, brown boxes that lined the walls.

The apostles finally reached the doorway, and Kluge instructed, "Find a seat." He also pointed to the only seats to be had. They were situated at the table in the center of the room.

Einar led Trixie to the center seating, moved the chairs nearer each other, and allowed Trixie to position into the seat first. He then followed after carefully maneuvering his body between Trixie's, the wood of the chair, and the table. Morton was bothered by the closeness of the twins, so he opted to sit at the head of the table before Kluge quickly stated, "The other side."

Acknowledging the command, Morton moved to the other side, although less willing to sit nearer the girl. And, the dolls were still intact, lying in a pile where Einar first dropped his cargo. The others copied the male twin's actions.

Kluge sat down and let out a hefty, professional "Ahem" in order to lure the attention of his guests. The ploy worked, and he did have the attention of all. Since he assumed that they needed employment, he was sure he would not have to use any other attention-getting tactics. Unfortunately, their attention was aided by their need to request advice from a man of law. Kluge would soon realize this.

Unable to hold in his patience anymore, Einar spoke. "Our theatrical careers have been stymied by a man known as Gertrude Sconch. He left town with our dignities slapped to his back. We are unemployed." Einar was emotionally devastated as he began to explain the situation that he patronized.

It was as Kluge suspected, but Einar's tone confused him. "So, how can I help?"

Nobody responded quickly to Kluge's question. He waited for further explanation. It was the girl who spoke. "We need to find him so that he can give us our jobs back."

This statement surprised Einar, especially because they had so often been confused by her mental abilities and inabilities. They were something he overlooked, only because the thought of being connected to someone so inept bothered him. Perhaps she was more aware than he had first thought for the thirty years of their lives. But then, after making a profound statement, Trixie found solace in a Rubik's cube that Einar had abruptly placed into her hand. He figured that her one moment of thoughtfulness was over. He was correct as she cautiously began turning the squares. This gave her utter enjoyment, although the insufferable outcome toyed with her emotions. Einar knew this and turned his attention to the sluggish conversation that began moments earlier.

Trixie's statement also surprised Kluge, as he did not expect the twins to want to work for anyone but him. Clearly, the twins would fit in with the myriad of circus entertainers.

"It's more than that, sir," Morton explained. He wanted to account for his opinion of the matter, since he was essentially left homeless after the ordeal.

Not being used to being addressed as sir by such as small person, Kluge sat up in his seat and leaned toward Morton who sat across from him. "Go on."

Morton, encouraged by the encouragement did go on. "I have been traveling with Ms. Sconch for many years."

Kluge's intermittent questioning interrupted him. "I thought this person was a man."

Einar chimed in. "His gender is a trivial matter. He is a man, but a woman. It is a very confusing matter."

"Fair enough, so this Ms. Sconch, did she? He? Steal from you? Did she? He? Pillage all of your belongings? I am confused by my role in this. Whatever that role may be." Kluge was recognizing that the twins waved him down in hopes to clarify their situation. He was bothered by the tedious walk and the inconvenient conversation being had.

Anxious to continue, Morton did not even address Kluge's questions. "I traveled with him and took part in all of the performances. This has gone on for years. Except this year, shortly after we arrived in this town, Gertrude Sconch met with Ms. Evelyn Smith."

Einar did the interrupting, "Sconch and Evelyn had a tryst?"

Morton scoffed at the idea. "I doubt they had a tryst, but they did meet. Your part in the show had a large part to do with that meeting. Anyhow," Morton continued, "he put me behind the scenes and kept me there until I met the twins. At first I was irate, but then I saw it as a brief escape from the mundane life that I lived."

Einar could not fully grasp what Morton had shared. "Did we not earn employment because of our abilities?" Einar was hurt and confused and wondered if his Aunt Evelyn was more capable of finding employment for them than them themselves. In that moment, his wondering was correct.

Also in that moment, Kluge was becoming increasingly perturbed by the soap box explanations that did not need his assistance at all. He focused on a segue that would close the current conversation and move it forward. "What did Sconch do?" He waited and then reiterated, perhaps more clearly. "His crime, what was his crime?"

Trixie, surprising Einar once again, was capable of overlooking the frustrating toy in her hand and focus on the questions. "He left."

"That's it? He left?" Kluge questioned. He was insistent upon getting to the bottom of this investigation. "So, um, what was the CRIME?" Kluge's tonnage was clear, concise, and entirely ineffective.

Einar used his best rhetoric to attempt to clearly show their emotional trials. "The crime was, Mr. Kluge," Einar stopped to think about how to portray Gertrude's actions as crime ridden. He continued, "Gertrude Sconch left us belittled and again, unemployed. Must we experience such strife? First the strike, now this. Is there any justice?"

Something Einar said prompted Kluge to move from the role of mediator into the role of a stern man of law. So he asked, "A strike? What strike?" Kluge was certainly more interested than ever because unfair employee practices had been his focus during part of his tenure. His interest would have been less than piqued if he had heard the gossip that swept through the town earlier that day. He did not, so this was tantalizing information for him.

"I organized a strike," Morton chimed. He was proud of his efforts.

"So, you organized...am I getting this right? Organized a strike, and then Sconch vanished?"

"Yes." Both Einar and Morton answered.

Kluge was still enthralled with this new bit of information. And, he, himself, had quite a bit of lawful information to share with everyone at the table. "Baldric Law prohibits striking workers in the city limits of Baldric. Your actions were unlawful. Unlawful at best. This event is inconceivable for this town, since work is scarce. Quite scarce. Employers do all that they can to ensure proper work environments for their employees. This is a fact. Revolting workers just do not fit in with the American dream." Kluge stopped and let this profound understanding seep into the brains, limited or not, of the three unemployed people that he reluctantly led to his family's storage warehouse. His family did, of course, need a place to store miscellaneous assemblages for the circus. Kluge then continued. He tried to mastermind the situation and to put a personal advantageous spin on the events that have unfolded before him. "There is nothing that I can do for you about the strike, unless I choose to turn you in. You'd be criminals."

Einar gasped, and Trixie let out a long-winded shriek.

Kluge's scare tactics worked. After their sudden reactions, Einar and Trixie both darted their eyes in the direction of the lawyer. Trixie was tearing up. Even though she may not have been the smartest person in that room that day, she sure did know what a criminal was. Kluge did not push the issue. He remained quiet, as did the others.

Just as the insufferable silence was beginning to calm the reactions of the twins, Bailiff Richards, Kluge's trusty security man who had impeccable timing, burst through the door. He heard a nearly inaudible clamor, probably the girl's shrill exclamation coming from the interior of the building and wanted to make sure that it was not another occurrence similar to the whole Tolbett ordeal. Bailiff Richards was unaware that Kluge's whereabouts were in that building. And, he actually had no idea that a significant meeting was transpiring inside the warehouse when he entered.

The bailiff stood at the door and sheepishly stared at the twins who returned the gaze. The bailiff could hardly see the midget, but he was thankful that he sighted Kluge, at the head of the table. "Oh! Do you…need me for anything?" he interrupted. His voice was stern and much louder than necessary. The latter was attributed to Bailiff Richard's slight hearing loss. Everything became more muffled, and his responses became embarrassingly more deafening.

Einar, Trixie, and Morton waited for Kluge's response, as Kluge had just explained that they were all essentially delinquents. "No Richards, I have this under control. It's all taken care of." Kluge finished and nodded at the door. He didn't need his own bailiff to stifle his plans.

The bailiff vaguely understood the cue and ambled away from the room that he just rushed into.

The sight of the handcuff toting man of law, even if the man was less than aware of his surroundings and really unaware of what was developing within the warehouse, startled the strikers, even more so than Kluge's comments about their situation. It was perfect timing for Kluge. Kluge began to speak, "You will work at the circus." Kluge had a plan. He continued, "Meet me tomorrow. Tomorrow morning. At the top of the hill. I will make sure that you fit in with the needs of the circus. It is my personal obligation to keep you," Kluge took a moment and stared Einar directly into his eyes and continued, "out of jail. So, half of your wages will be garnished to the Law Office of Kluge and Kluge for its services, as you cannot," Kluge paused again and eyed the female, who was still grasping the Rubik's Cube, and then he eyed the male twin before continuing, "pay in any other form. And, leave the dolls. They must be mine."

Einar was oddly suspicious of Kluge's last comment about the dolls and feared for their innocence. But, Einar's confusion was overridden by a feeling of relief and freedom. He was alive and was going to be indebted to someone else. It was what he aspired for; it was part of the American dream. He would work to pay his debts, even if his debtor was Kluge.

TWELVE

The Master of the Hiring

The next day, everyone, which included Einar, Trixie, and Morton, arrived at the bottom of Tolbett's Hill early enough to see the organized chaos. Dirt wafted through the air, as the trucks rolled into town and stopped sporadically along the dry plains and rolling hills that eventually would transform into a field of colorful entertainment. Each year, the circus overlooked the less than elaborate town of Baldric, with the painstaking shambles of houses and shacks positioned so picturesque at the bottom of the hill. Tolbett's Hill, unlike the day prior, did not look desolate or eerie.

The trio trudged up the hill. They quickened their paces more than usual. Once at the top, Einar and Trixie, with Morton trailing, marched to the trailer that was located off to the side of the mess of the dirt mounds. This was where, as Kluge would say, "The magic happens." Nobody dare questioned Kluge about what he meant, but Einar was sure that the marionettes had been escorted into the only structure standing amidst the trucks and the mist of dirty air. Einar reminded himself to not worry about such trivial matters; he was there for business. Morton had the same idea, business, as he marched up the stairs and pulled his fist to pound a mass of air into the door. Just then, Kluge, fitted in aviator styled shades, opened the door and relieved it of a brutal pounding.

Kluge, wearing his most formal knickers and smoking a pipe, exited his trailer and brushed past Morton as he stomped down the stairs. "Follow," was the only direction he gave. And, the twins, along with Morton, respectfully abided. Trixie was happy that Kluge did not wear a dress, and he did not end his demand with "Ahora"; that word, as well as the she-man, still perplexed the girl.

Kluge headed around the trailer and led the twins and the midget to meet a plethora of other freaks and genetic mutants, all of whom held the hope of a future with the traveling circus. The twins and Morton soon joined the masquerade when Kluge aided their direction by a sweep of his arm. Not waiting for any conversation to cease, Kluge spoke sternly. "Line up," he yelled. "Line up now," he yelled again. Now listening, all the interviewees scampered behind the makeshift trailer and lined up, firing squad style, at Kluge's request. Bearded women and midgets and dwarfs surrounded the twins and Morton; it was an appropriate scene under those circumstances. The homeless and any other spectacle that met the restrictions of the circus and lived near the town of Baldric seemed to be in attendance that day.

Kluge walked past the interesting row and inspected all of the anxious applicants' peculiarities and oddities. It was the formal interview, freaks pitted against freaks, the weird against weird, and the twins and Morton standing as if they were seemingly normal in this crowd. Easing his oral fixation, Kluge placed the pipe aside and then placed a slim into his mouth and lit it as he approached the twins and Morton. The burning cherry pointed at their noses. Trixie, fearing the heat that emitted from the fire, moved back suddenly. This abrupt movement caused Einar to nearly lose his balance.

"You're not tightrope walkers. No balance." Kluge chuckled at his observance, adding "clumsy" to his mental opinion of the twins.

Almost sad at Kluge's statement, Trixie let out an "Hmmppphh," much like she often wanted to respond to Einar.

She, though, could only imagine what a tightrope was.

Kluge soon paced beyond the twins to affix his attention on two bearded women. One was certainly going to leave with disappointment. The one on his right maintained a beard of high quality, according to Kluge. "Stand over there," he pointed, "next to the trailer." The long flowing strands of grayish color cascaded gently along the woman's neck as she moved next to the trailer. The other one, who stood to the left of Kluge, was asked to leave; her beard was a bit more scarce than Kluge would have liked, and its age did not lend to the same distinction as the other's beard had. Kluge was the expert.

The expert interviewer then passed the myriad of small people as he pointed down the line. "Dance for me," he demanded. The pawns danced, and Kluge, after careful watching of each display, generated his opinion of each applicant. When he made his decision, he pointed at each of the people appropriate for the circus and exclaimed the good news. "Welcome to the circus," he bellowed. This continued as he approached Morton.

Kluge made his way in front of Morton, who was anxiously awaiting the man's approval. "Jiggle like this." Kluge shimmied his body and looked quite ludicrous doing so. Morton mirrored the man's actions, although the midget was much more graceful. Kluge tilted his head to the left. Morton tilted his head to the right. And after a thoughtful investigation, Kluge welcomed Morton into the family business. After that embarrassing and contemplative display, Kluge moved onto the next set of disadvantaged people. He then pointed to the variety of fingerless, legless, and armless homeless folk, all of whom traveled like a group of nomads, although many of them had limited abilities because of dismembered limbs and such. "Stand on your heads," he demanded. Although the request was somewhat demeaning and caused difficulty for those without arms, all of the applicants adhered to Kluge's wills to the best of their abilities.

Kluge then pointed to those he found the most favorable for the circus and told them to wait near the bearded woman. Sighs of relief and content echoed down the hill as many of the applicants found solace in the idea that they were, finally, employed. This was especially special for those who lived life under many disadvantaged circumstances.

The day was even marvelous for Kluge who stopped his assessments to exclaim, "This is incredible! Just incredible!" He was pleasantly pleased at the hoard of talent and thought twice about summoning the twins. Kluge sighed and then continued his endeavor, whittling down the crowd until only the Smith twins were left standing. Kluge paced back and forth in front of the twins.

Because Einar realized that Kluge was internally questioning his and Trixie's role in the circus, he thought to showcase his and Trixie's own aerobatic maneuvers. He abruptly pushed Trixie onto the dirt ground and followed her fall. As they fell, Einar maneuvered his body into a ball and rolled. The movement forced Trixie to haphazardly do the same. They tumbled through the dust cloud created by the collapse.

The newfound employees found the awkward site quite entertaining, and a rash of laughter and finger-pointing spread through the crowd, including Kluge. As Trixie erratically waved her arms to clear the air particles, she grasped her breath lost by the unexpected plummet. Einar turned to the girl and asked, "Are you okay?"

Trixie failed to respond. Kluge was also having difficulty responding to the sight he had just witnessed.

Einar figured that his actions did not aid Kluge in his decision because of his and Trixie's horrendous, inabilities that lacked showmanship and skill. Somber and disappointed, Einar lifted Trixie off of the ground. Trixie, too, felt saddened. "We might be criminals," Einar stated to Trixie who was too busy wiping the dirt off of her face to listen.

Kluge again paced back and forth. As his attention fell upon the twins, he recognized their desperation. "Go!" he ordered as he pointed to the others who he welcomed into the circus. Kluge was certain that Einar and Trixie were going to be beneficial to the circus, if only because of their genetically exceptional anatomy. They were twins, two-of-a-kind, after all.

Einar noticed two things after this moment. First, Kluge's Traveling Circus had become their rightful employer, if only because of Kluge's nepotism for the twins. Second, Kluge had an aversion to anyone considered a dwarf, perhaps because of the disproportionate body, and kindly sent all seven of the dwarfish figures away. That was all Einar could recall in his moment of success.

Interrupting the excitement, the rumble of the trucks and cranes resounded through the putrid Baldric air. The noise caused Kluge to have to scream at the crowd, which had diminished solely to those who he anticipated on hiring. "Return tomorrow to this dump," he advised. Kluge evidently accepted the reality that the circus was mounted atop the dirt covered garbage pits.

The twins concocted their departure after Kluge reputably vanished from the nether of the trailer. They turned to search for Morton whose attention had been diverted from his fortunate circumstance to Molly, one of the new hires.

Poised behind the trailer, the two midgets lusting after one another were found by the twins right before Morton planned on shifting the girl's shirt to the side to view and massage her perky bosom. Molly, the staunch prude that she was, would not have let that happen, but her fascination of the man midget did show upon her face. She stared into Morton's big brown eyes that were hidden by a pair of over-sized glasses worn for the prestigious job interview. The glasses that made Morton look like quite the educated individual also allowed him to capture Molly's true beauty, even if she was cockeyed and he couldn't figure out which eye to peer into. Every time she peered through the large glass spectacles, a bright smile filled the girl's countenance. She liked what she saw, even if the image was a bit obscured.

The approaching twins startled the girl and the midget who had to do many adjustments as soon as he spotted them. Molly, unable to see them approaching, leaned toward Morton to lay a wet, sloppy kiss upon his cheek, but Morton's surprise provoked him to jerk and caused Molly to lay a wet one on his ear.

"Morton, it is time," Einar preached, "to leave this blessed site and return home."

Molly, confused by the interruption necessarily asked, "Are those your parents?" No excuse could be made for her misunderstanding, considering Einar and Trixie could not ever procreate together and birth a child or even a midget. Plus, Morton was obviously a man beyond his thirties. The graying locks were the first sign.

"No sweetheart, they are my roommates," Morton responded. He did not want his newfound darling to know he was a mere stowaway. Anyhow, the fully enamored girl might not understand that the twins' misfortune over the past few days had been almost entirely Morton's fault.

The midgets stood hand in hand, and experienced a sheer osmosis of yearning. They awaited the next cue from the father like figure. It did not take long. "Trix and I are departing," Einar noted. It was a succinct statement, and one that Morton and his little lick of love understood quite clearly.

To clarify any misunderstanding, Morton turned to the girl, "If you would like, I could walk you home." Unaware as to where Molly lived, although fearful that she would not be able to find her home, Morton became quite an officious man of chivalry. Unbeknownst to him, Molly could see well enough to take herself home, if she felt like trudging through the neighboring town several miles northward.

"I came with," Molly interrupted herself to look around the vacant hills to find the large yellow bus that smuggled the young girl into the town of Baldric. She was left behind. "Oh," she continued.

As Molly's good eye scanned the area, she twisted and turned to catch up with her seeing device. To no avail, none of the other applicants were within sight. Betwixt the trailer and the harassing dust clouds, the two midgets and tumbling twins stood alone on the hill.

"I presume you are immobilized in this lovely town." Einar was anxious to return home and revel in his newfound position, whatever that position would be in the circus, so he was sadly sarcastic with the abandoned. He did not even offer his rustic home as an overnight abode. Since the fear that the law was after him had subsided, it prompted Einar to lose all sense of empathy.

"You're not stuck here; come with us," Trixie insisted. After witnessing the harsh display of her brother, she finally had reason to speak above her brother's defiant, cocky nature.

With a nod and a smile, Molly, still lovingly attached to the much older Morton agreed to the latter persuasion. And with that, the trio, now a quartet, returned to the Smith's home.

THIRTEEN

Learning of the Past

A week separated from them from their introduction to the workforce, and Einar and Trixie were becoming experienced wage seekers. Einar led Trixie on their way to what Einar deemed, "our real job", as if the theater production was not real. The twins, and even Morton, felt that they had truly found their calling. Einar was cleverly aware that his and Trixie's strength was their genetic disposition. Only Trixie understood that her and Einar's weakness was their genetic disposition. But, she lumbered up Tolbett's Hill alongside Einar anyhow.

"Where do we go first?" Morton questioned. He, hand in hand with the lovely Molly who did not succumb to Morton's less than gentile gestures, was weaving in and out of crowds of people, most of whom were professionals, beelining towards their rightful places.

Einar pointed to the trailer where he spotted many others from the day prior. He then turned to Trixie and spoke, "This is our calling. Fear nothing; just follow my lead." The latter of his statement was literal and figurative as he pulled Trixie closer to the steps of the trailer.

"Who's calling?" Trixie inquired, not understanding what Einar meant.

The male ignored his sister, a common response. So, Trixie allowed Einar to pull her up the hill as she witnessed the hustle and bustle occurring so early that morning.

The first day of circus work was always the most tedious. The auspicious groups of psychics, the trapeze acts, the clowns, midgets, stagehands, animals, and weird oddities abounded to fulfill their quest in providing the best form of amusement for the crowds and masses seeking mindless entertainment. With the tents erected in glorious colors and the subsequently more miniature stands of lemonade and hotdogs situated around the rented fields, Baldric's most prominent hill was a desert's oasis for the depraved. But, the abrasive practices of the first day, precedent to the widespread unveiling of the circus, always included a myriad of mistakes and dangerous entanglements usually attributed to the sluggish contortionists.

With two or more weeks of idleness between performances, the circus acts and performances were always a bit rustic. With the newcomers, who were always hired within the limits of Baldric, the practices were painstakingly difficult. Rehearsals from dusk to dawn always alleviated the budding problems, unless they revolved around the synchronized swimmers. It was rumored that the circus once lost an entire synchronized swimming team in the shallow waters at the makeshift pool because of confusion with the counts that refrained the members of the team from surfacing. Afterward, the pool work was only done during performances, and the team, which was once hailed as nearly Olympic caliber, was likened to a team of decent swimmers who could, at times, coordinate movements fairly well, in more of an unsynchronized fashion. People didn't go to the circus to see the synchronized act anyhow.

With several new acts and a multitude of new members vying for momentary fame with the swimming team, it was going to be a trying time for Kluge and the circus. While being interviewed by Melanie Jefferson, Kluge was aware of his barriers and noted, "We, the circus and I, will prevail. Prevail indeed."

When Einar led Trixie up the hill, the same thought as Kluge's surfaced. Einar's "we" that would prevail was he and Trixie. Only time would tell, but nothing could change the fate of the twins, especially because of Einar's stubbornness and instantaneous gratitude to Kluge and his acquittal.

As they reached the summit of the hill top, Einar, Trixie, Morton and Molly were included among the bunch who stomped up the metal incline into the trailer after beholding the vibrant scenes of the extravaganza. Inside of Kluge's secondary office, the visuals were anything but visually arresting. It was a much more dingy scene than what lay beyond the windows of the twelve by thirty structure that was upheaved, with limited damage, from the dump that lay below it.

The crowd assembled in groups outside of the small structure. Anyone shorter than four feet, the pocket people- as Kluge would refer to them, entered the trailer, per Kluge's request, and were then assigned to go to specific locations. "There, it's in the little tent, that speck of color. Out of the window." He pointed as he directed the abnormally short people to the meeting tent where the midgets would be assigned clowns, greeters, ticket sales, or psychics. Looking slightly earthward, Kluge motioned the miniature people out of his office to make way for the more significant acts. Morton followed Kluge's prompting. Anxiously, he left with his own odd fascination with nineteenth century English peasants and hoped for a job as a pickpocket. Eventually though, he understood what a circus was, and he had to settle for a less than respectable trade, one that included little or no pilfering.

As the door swung open from the miniature humans exiting, it trapped, only briefly, a brisk rush of fresh air when the twins entered. They were alone with Kluge. When the door closed, Kluge addressed the twins. "See the top of the hill? The very top." He waited for the twins to maneuver themselves closely enough to the window to peer out of it, and then he continued without any verbal affirmation. He knew that the twins, although slow at times, were not blind. "Go halfway and stop. Your tent is situated next to Madam Bovine's. If you have trouble finding its location, look for the traveling musicians who seek out charities from the new employees. Then, ask them. I am too busy, way too busy, to become your personal guide. As far as your act is concerned, do what you like; just make me some money. Lots of money. You will understand what I mean by this at the end of the day once we are all prepared. Prepared for the big day."

Kluge was almost excited to see the outcome of this strategical move on his part. Proper advertising of the twins would surely encourage the members of Baldric to view the twins as animals, or more appropriately, as oddities in a cage. Only this time, the members of Baldric would be able to maintain up close contact with them, something they could have only done in The Law Office of Kluge and Kluge and in the church all because of Lola's selfishness. Kluge, a witness of the town's fascination of the twins on the day of the reading, knew that the clamoring would infiltrate the conversations throughout the town if the people heard that he had the twins caged, and accessible to view like a fine piece of art or a train wreck, whichever they deemed.

Dismissed from the trailer, the twins were guided by the erupting sounds of musical instruments. They journeyed through the maze of upright structures. What would have been a simple task for others was seemingly difficult for the twins as they, together, climbed up a slight incline and stepped succinctly through the dirt worn paths naturally plowed by anxious circus folk and spectators that arrived each year for ninety-nine years straight after a two year pause due to a pending strike that was actually favorable for the workers. Of course, just like any law in Baldric, the non-striking clause was determined after this occurrence, ironic for the twins and their circumstance. Eager to begin his endeavor and fully accept his circumstance, Einar led

Trixie through the circular labyrinth.

The worn paths guided the twins directly to their circus home, but instead of entering the tattered tent situated next to one of the most alluring places in the world of the circus, the Tent of Fortunes, Einar and Trixie schlepped through the intricate weave of trails. As they walked, they peeped into the miscellaneous structures and viewed the bustling activities of the circus folk.

The first stop for the twins, in part to avoid the meddling musicians, was at the venerated Museum of the Kluge Circus. Situated in a brown tent, ornate with large white stripes and topped with a large white flag, the museum offered historical information and current statistics of the world of Kluge's Traveling Circus. Einar and Trixie walked in, passing the entranceway waving its heavy tarp in rapid succession to the wind's suggestions. Knowing the freedom that entailed, Einar spoke, "If this is work, we have been led astray by Lola. This is sensational." Considering everything that Einar and Trixie had experienced and seen that day, Einar kept his emotions relatively intact.

Trixie did not keep her emotions intact. With the brief reference to Lola, Trixie's weariness and emotion had succumbed to her anxiousness. "I miss Lola," she said. It was not what she said but how she said it that made Einar proud. The girl had finally referred to her mother as Lola.

Although proud of Trixie's terminology, Einar nearly shunned the statement in general. But, he decided to inquire into her state of being, as her state of being was always his concern. "Why?"

"I am tired," she answered honestly. Trixie had never had so many responsibilities, and the idea of a nice, simple, confined life made her happy. With Lola around, her life was confined, and simple, and nice. She realized that her choices were limited and her mornings were long as Einar led her through the tent.

The tent was dark, yet the natural light that shone in with

every flap of the tarp allowed for the twins to see the bales of hay aligned in front of a large void of space at the back of the tent. Because the more antique artifacts were raided by a rival circus, the museum had to resort to creating a moving pictorial of the history Kluge's circus until the looted supplies could be replenished. Baldric Law refused the return of confiscated items, even if the items were confiscated unlawfully outside of the town. And if the circus knew anything, it was the Law of Baldric.

As the twins walked into the tent, the movie had already begun. The stream of picture diagonally turned from the ceiling of the tent.

Trixie was discombobulated by all of the aesthetically appealing sights and the euphoric sound. "Where are we?" she asked. The darkness had confused Trixie, who suffered from the ailment of forgetfulness. Moments before, she clearly read the sign lit with bright red bulbs outside the tent. The sign was clear: Circus Museum.

In normal movie spectator fashion, Einar hushed a "Shhhh" to his twin as he became immediately entranced by the moving picture that scrolled across the giant makeshift screen. He led Trixie, also fascinated by the sight, to the center bale of hay. His unknown force coerced her to settle into the bale next to him. Within an instant, Einar understood the difference between the live art of the theater and the produced art of the movie. He liked what he saw.

Trixie had not thought to compare the two. She was too busy distracting herself. After fidgeting to find comfort, Trixie, eventually paying attention to the screen, laid her head upon her brother's shoulder. Although the image was a bit askew from her vantage point, Trixie found the pictures intriguing until her eyes closed, and eventually she screened only the darkness of her mind.

While the girl was asleep, the sound boomed through the vacant tent. The girl missed out viewing the secrets and riveting facts about the circus from years past. She missed the voice explaining that the circus was once a symbol of freedom-individually and nationally. She would have liked that. Even if his sister was not, Einar was attentive, and he was intent on understanding what came before him before he was even a thought in his mother's uterus.

"And then," the movie projected, "tough times fell upon the circus."

Einar inched up on his seat while trying to not startle the other twin who was snuggled closely into his chest. "Business became competition, and competition became fierce. People wanted bigger and better, and more. The circus, already a spectacle from years past, became a mere memory in the minds of the visitors who became grown and believed in the concept of the American dream." Einar was fascinated with this facet of information and was beginning to slowly understand such aspects of American life.

The toil, the misleading expectations, the fake happiness that combined to create a normal, American life was what Einar yearned. It was acceptance from society, and he knew that to exist successfully, without question, he too would have to follow those expectations set forth by all of society. He needed to make a home, provide for his family, obey the law, and be the Einar Smith that society would accept in order to truly feel the fake satisfaction of life. Lola did it and masked her own grief day after day, so why couldn't he? Except, he was sure to handle life much better than Lola. Einar glanced at Trixie, who surely expected his guidance. After much thought, he realized that he, above all else, wanted a taste, a sliver of that distorted American dream.

An incessant flash of light, which startled both the slumbering twin and the thoughtful male, blazed across the screen. Popular music blared through the speakers. And then the voice roared, "But now." The flashes began again. They jolted Trixie from her more comfortable position and caused her to sit upright. The sights of the bright lights and the booming sound mesmerized the simple mind.

The narrator screamed, "The circus is better than ever!" It was a critical statistic necessary for Einar's interest.

Just as the invisible speaker finished, glorious pictures of all individuals-large and small-, stage acts, and assorted edibles flashed intermittently with the bright lights. The synchronicity of the music and the scenes were proper explanations for what the circus symbolized, which was a collaboration of business and entertainment to provide the peons of society with sheer, gratuitous enjoyment, with the inclusion of flashing lights, interesting sounds, fascinating smells, and amazing sights.

Einar was ready to be a part of this amazing feat that transcended life itself, and he was even more excited to join the ranks of society instead of being a mere pawn to entertainment, like he and Trixie had been as cast members for the exanimate "Modern Times". The circus, though, was much bigger than and more modern than the theater. And, the times were different. The future and the history of Baldric, as it appeared to Einar, who was engrossed by the whole scenario, was actually the place upon which he set foot early that morning. Not Tolbett's Hill, although an intriguing story, the circus, it was the circus that was bigger than life with more opportunities for the town, and nothing better could reflect the life that Einar wanted for himself and his twin.

When the movie ended, Trixie, a bit confused by the lights and sounds, found it necessary to ask, "Did I miss anything?" She usually did, and this time was no different.

"You missed a lot," Einar answered and then added, "I missed a lot." A tear rolled down his face as he looked up to the apex of the tent in hopes to drain his eyes of their flood and drain his mind of his sheltered memory that did miss more than he could even recognize.

FOURTEEN

A Residual Fear is Cast

Clearly, Einar was appreciative of the opportunity. He was a part of the circus. Besides, the circus had to be a better place than prison confinement. With this understanding, Einar was eager to begin work, even if his entire being, including that of his sister, was prostituted out by none other than Loki Kluge. It was a part of the satisfaction that Einar longed for, regardless of the situation and the overwhelming threat of prison confinement that led them there. Plus, Einar figured and knew that he did owe the man who he thought so little of only weeks earlier.

"We must visit our tent. And, let us put forth a show that will enthrall all who visit. We must become a part of this, even if we die trying." Einar was ready for all that life, or at least life at the circus, had to offer.

"I'm still sleepy," Trixie whispered. It was all Trixie could afford to suggest.

"We, my dear Trix," Einar began to explain. He wanted his excitement to seep into the veins of the girl who would be sure to enjoy the adventures of the circus and all it had to offer, so he continued, "we can sleep when we join mother. Until then, we must make up for the multitude of years we have not been a part of this." Einar's arms spread wide. The limb knocked Trixie in her bosom that jutted into its path. The "this" he referred to was not actually the circus; it was life. It was the life that had been stripped from the twins the moment their mother held them hostage from society in an effort to keep them all to herself and to shelter them. Einar, more than ever, wondered why the tramp would have done such a thing, but he would not ever question it in front of his sister for fear that their strong bond would be broken because of mere opposition in relation to the woman they used to call mother.

"But, I just want to rest for a moment." Trixie unexpectedly interrupted her brother's thoughts.

"No!" Einar revolted. He was saddened by the interruption. He was happy for himself and amazingly, just as Lola had sheltered the twins from others, Einar was doing the same. He sheltered Trixie from her own desires, even if she did not know what all of them were.

The rush of excitement from the performers and all employees of the circus fluttered throughout the air as the scene became increasingly like that of a true circus. The sights and sounds, like those seen and heard on the big tent screen came to life and became more animated. The hustle inspired the male twin while it made the female one even more fatigued. It was hypnotic, a sensory overload for the female. But, Trixie eventually surrendered her basic need to succumb to Einar's wishes, just like she always had.

"Where's our tent?" she inquired. She was usually unable to find anything without the aid of her brother.

"I am leading us there," he remarked. He led them just like he always had.

After their brief conversation, the twins distinguished Morton, who was eyeing the buttocks of a taller woman walking ahead of him. Morton was definitely invading her personal space, but she remained unknowing. Trixie wanted to call out, but the pace of the woman that Morton was stalking was much faster than hers and Einar's pace. She did wonder though, "What about Molly?"

Einar shrugged, and Trixie felt the force of his motion, a motion that answered the question. Einar was more focused on less trivial matters.

When the twins passed the big top, the excitement discharging from within the vinyl structure was enough to make Trixie just a bit eager. "What're we going to do?" she asked, now peering through the large curtain that created the barrier between the outside world and the crazed world of the circus.

Einar had no answer, so the twins continued onward. They were led by the traveling sounds of the bellow of the saxophone and the chimes of the tambourine. They screamed for change. When Einar and Trixie arrived at their tent, they entered. In the small absence of space, that was lit dimly by the overhead, escaping sunlight, a faint echo sounded throughout as Trixie yelled, "Is this it?" She then felt necessary to comment on the meager size of the place. "This is small, too small." She learned the repetition technique from listening to Kluge.

Einar wondered about her comment. "Too miniscule for what?" he questioned.

"For," and at that moment, Trixie tugged upon Einar's upper body and pulled him from place to place. She then continued her statement, "us to move." She finally felt the soul of the circus creep in.

"So what do you ascertain we do in this place?"

After taking a moment to understand what a certain was, Trixie tugged more fervently on Einar's entire body. She twirled herself and her brother around with utmost command. "Dance," she demanded. The demand likened the directives that she heard Kluge yell so passionately at the interview, and her movements likened those she learned from Gertrude, but now, it was less forced and even a bit enjoyable. Of course, Trixie was the one to experience such joyousness, unlike Einar, whose body thrashed from one end of the tent to the other. The bit lasted a few minutes, until Trixie's leg entwined with Einar's. The entanglement caused the twins to lose their footing and tumble to the ground. This seemed to be commonplace for the two. Unlike the first time that something similar happened, both the twins were laughing hysterically on the ground.

"I have not laughed so intensely in…" Einar thought for a moment and continued, "for quite a while." The harshness of their reality settled into his mind. Their lives were much different than they had prior to their mother's death. It was bittersweet, and Einar was almost resentful of his mother's choices, except for the one that ended in her pleasant pregnancy with the twins.

Both twins lolled on the ground with their heads positioned upside down toward the opening of the tent. They were soon surrounded by an assemblage of colorful and unique people, people from the circus and beyond.

Understanding the glances that looked upon her as a naked muse, Trixie covered up her body with one arm and used her free arm to cover up Einar's. In the midst of the circus and the surrounding people watching, Trixie felt like an outcast. Her personal, innocent moment was spoiled by the glares of the onlookers. She was certainly going to have a rough time at her new place of employment.

Einar, accepting of his position in the circus, lifted his arm that was covered with brown soil and strands of hay; he waved to the crowd.

The wave prompted the crowd to applaud the efforts of the twins.

With this moment of accreditation, Einar was pleased with the acceptance, yet Trixie was abhorred; her hand moving to cover her face showed that. Her eyes that peered out of the space in her fingers drew forth a precipitation of sadness, drowning her memory of elation. She too knew that life was much unlike it had been when her mother was alive.

The crowd soon disappeared, and with an effort to become more attentive to his sister's feelings and needs, Einar attempted to relax her and dulcify the sensation of betrayal, although he had no idea why she had become so distraught. The stares that Trixie noticed on rare occasions made her increasingly uncomfortable in her own skin. And, she was weary. The more she looked at her body and at Einar's and then at the bodies of the people around the town, Trixie slowly became cognizant of her, their, differences. It was that awareness that caused the anxiety, and it was that awareness that Einar tried to relieve Trixie of as he led her outside of the tent.

"Trix, we are going to be stars. Look at this. Look at our surroundings," he encouraged. Einar expatiated his expressive proclamation while they stood outside of their brightly lit tent rightfully branded EINIX. The twins were affixed with this designation after Kluge used his most ingenious advertising ploy to allure patrons into the tent. Upon watching the twins twist and tumble with utmost struggle, Kluge found the title to be quite fitting; they were after all, nearly the true duplication of one person, one soul, and their physical struggles mimicked the actions that normal humans found to be less strenuous. The twins and their mutual attachment to one another were transcending the philosophical realm of free will. Neither was free without the other, and neither could ever be free with the other. It was a conundrum that the circus wanted to aptly display.

Trixie glanced at the sign in utter amazement and realized briefly, "What is an Einix?" she asked. It was a word that she was not accustomed to.

Einar solicited his explanation, "That is us. Our names have converged to make one. Is that not clever? Kluge, as I hope to become, is the master of business." Einar's initial reaction to Kluge, the witty lawman, was less than favorable, but the man's useful tactics involving the carnival, vindicated Einar's newfound respect for him, as Einar had so awkwardly described to his twin just moments earlier. It was an unexplainable moment for Einar, but he was willing to annul every bit of negativity that included his first impression of the lawyer.

Trixie, who had always thought of Kluge as a funny, greasy fellow, obviously enjoyed her birth name and the individuality it rendered. "But we are two people. Why do they think we are one person?" Trixie slowly felt her eccentricity seep away from her being, just as she had been stripped of her name, the one thing she couldn't share with her brother. For once, she realized that her differences defined her individuality. She just didn't want people staring.

Einar tried to negotiate with his sister's feelings and apprehension. "Well, we, as recognized by the circus, need to become one person." Einar knew the appointment behind the plan, especially since he always attempted to grapple with the idea that they, the twins, were seemingly one person with duel personalities. If only Trixie could understand, they could dominate the circus arena. "We, as Einix, shall rise beyond this; it will change us and encourage us. We shall never be the same again."

"And that's a good thing?" Trixie could not grasp this idea that Einar spoke of so fervently. She, in a deniable fashion, appreciated her life even if Einar was, at times, protective of not only her being but of her mind and aspirations. Einar needed to protect them of that life that they led, and Trixie assumed that he would.

Einar obviously thought that the circus had their best interest at hand. But before he could respond to Trixie's questioning, a few brawny men, carrying a large brown box, shoved past the twins who were still mesmerized by the sign that hung above the entrance. Wanting to see what was hidden in the surprising package, Einar propelled Trixie, brushing the sides of the colorful tarp, beyond the aperture into the tent.

The brown box unveiled a large Plexiglas structure. It was meant for protection of the twins, as Kluge, who, with the aid of Madam Bovine, knew that the twins could become something spectacular. Any harm to the twins could also harm his position with the circus and in the town, and he was sure to ensure that that would not occur.

As Einar spoke to Trixie, it was mere gibberish. She was too fixated on the package that she could neither understand nor respond to her brother. Once the men turned the structure upright, Trixie became involved with looking for an image in the structure, but she could not find one. The dim of the light was not bright enough to mirror a reflection. Upon another disappointing investigation, the girl found that the structure's positioning in the middle of the tent depleted the open space. "How are we going to dance or even move?" Trixie looked upon her brother for a sound answer as she had become quite accustomed to doing.

"We will just have to revise our routine to accommodate the situation." Einar tugged upon Trixie's arm in a playful manner. When he turned to show off their infamous twisting, Trixie did not turn with him. It caused nothing but pain for the twin who wanted to do nothing but sulk. Einar, again, attempted to mitigate the circumstances. "We, Trix, are hired to do a job, and we must do it. Do you not want to be a star?"

It was a question asked way too often for the female twin, yet she wasn't sure how to answer. "I don't want to be in a cage like an animal," she explained. Perhaps she was smarter than she led on, yet it was not a perception that led her to believe this. It was a distant, childhood memory that recalled her emotions.

The structure had reminded Trixie of the cages in the pet store that she visited once when she and Einar were ten. Their mother promised them a pet if they assured her that they would not roam the streets when she was at work.

She remembered the conversation that her mother had with

Einar. Lola explained, "Einar, don't you dare leave. If you do, I will crush your dream of having a pet and something else to look after when I am away."

Einar had always been slightly deviant, but he figured that a pet would reel in Trixie's attention so that she would not be so curious about everything that he was doing. After a week of the twins obliging to her wishes, Lola took them to the store that sold animals. Trixie was entirely thrilled by the idea, especially because she thought that she had coerced Einar to accept the agreement. Of course, it was not Trixie's encouragement; he would have been more content winding through the cobblestone streets filled with migrant wage seekers and unemployed rubes. It was one of the few times that he gave into Trixie's desires. He learned his lesson.

The brief trip to the store should have been ordinary for the twins, although they rarely left their home and rarely traveled to any business within walking distance. Lola gave them orders and kept them in line. Yet, as soon as Trixie entered and saw the caged animals, she began to scream. She declared that the smell and the sights of the screeching animals disgusted her. The constant shrieking and blaring caused an uproar among most of the animals. One of the parrots, an efficient and intelligent species, unlocked its cage and flew directly into Einar's face. It bit the tip of his nose. From that point on, Einar despised animals, and Trixie despised cages, and neither was granted a pet, that was, until Morton came into town.

"We, obviously, are not animals," Einar was actually wrong in his assumption. He continued, "And we, obviously, are not going to be caged." Again, his assumption was incorrect. "This is for our protection, so you must alleviate those memories of the pet store," he explained. Although the twins were quite different, Einar often did know what Trixie was thinking.

"Fine," she retorted, knowing that she had no escape. She had finally agreed to the arrangement, even if she did not have any say.

It was a feeling that she was used to.

Throughout Trixie's catechism of her brother and his and the box's intentions, the structure became enshrouded with an adjustable, mechanical cloth. The movement of the cloth was going to be instigated by the coin box. It was a decadent peep show that Kluge designed himself, as part of the preparation for Lola's death, although Kluge wasn't aware of the upcoming death. Lola knew that this was the fate of her twins; Einar had no idea that Lola even thought about the fate of the twins before she died. She just didn't realize that the twins were going to be distracted by the theater of sin. Regardless, her plan was coming to fruition.

The tent was usurped of its glorious spaciousness, and outside, Bailiff Richards situated himself to practice a run through for the following evening. He was to ensure that only one person at a time could search for the entertainment beyond the enclosure, and that one person had to pay with real money. The design and overall plan was financially genius, even if Richards, unaware of his deafening state and blinding right eye, was oblivious too much of the unlawful behavior at the circus. Regardless, Kluge and his family were surely going to benefit.

And, if Einar had any say, he was surely going to benefit as well. Trixie would reap the rewards along with him, even if her emotional state was less than spirited.

FIFTEEN

The Fates will Have Their Day

After an exhaustive day when night settled in and the dusk disappeared into the depths of the darkness, Einar deemed the day over. He and Trixie schlepped down the sidewalk toward their home. Morton, finding an unexpected aversion with Baldric's most notorious prostitute, did not join the twins in the journey. And Molly, well, she was lucky if she remembered her own name. She would have to learn how to utilize sweet and stupid to function in life. Anyhow, as Trixie, the more considerate of the twins, left the nearly deserted bazaar, she was not at all concerned about the whereabouts of Morton, nor did she care about the whereabouts of Molly. Trixie was just determined to leave that place, that evil, devastating place. Her self-doubt had given her something else on which to focus. So, they walked in peace. They walked in quiet.

The silence of their travels allowed Trixie's fading memories to pacify her conscience, as did the brief "Psst…" she recognized just as they turned the corner of the main street onto a more discrete lane. Trixie, hearing the call, stopped Einar from forcing forward.

"Did you hear that?" she asked.

Einar looked around the desolate street lit by only one blinking streetlight that hummed its last breath. He then searched for a sound other than the gasps of the light. "No. My ears have not devoured any sound," Einar answered.

They stepped forward again, and the noise returned. This time, it was more exaggerated. "Psssssssst."

Einar halted their progress. "Something is now audible." He looked around, certain of Trixie's first assessment.

"Over here," the voice whispered. It coaxed Trixie and Einar to look around.

Trixie looked in the direction where she presumed "here" was.

"No...here," the voice persisted.

Einar looked "here" and focused on the oak posted mailbox that bent over the entranceway of Old Man McCormick's lane, as labeled by the street sign. "There," Einar directed as he pointed toward the receptacle that was surrounded by enlarge grasses and a man who was decorated in the finest replica of Civil War costuming and a green fedora embellished with a gray, fluffy feather. The outfit was intended to blend in with the surrounding foliage in case somebody other than the twins passed the lane. The man was hunched over.

At first, Trixie did not see the man, his costuming intentions were perhaps a bit too clever. The girl wondered how a mailbox could make such sounds, but she was mistaken as Old Man McCormick stood upright from his stoop. In a "tada" fashion, the man held his arms upright and flailed them fully to reveal himself to the twins. "Here," he motioned. He waited for both Trixie's and Einar's acknowledgment and ordered, "Follow me."

Peeping a quizzical look at Trixie, Einar shrugged his shoulders and advanced closer to the man. Einar dragged Trixie with him. She did not oppose her brother's movement. The weird, hunched man who hid in the bushes entertained Trixie enough to erase her memory of the recent events of the day. Plus, she thought that he had an odd resemblance with Kluge and Gertrude.

The old man, who actually was not that old, entered the

twins' lives that night. He was wholly unaware that he maintained any similitude with the aforementioned men who already impacted the twins. If he had known this, he wouldn't have believed it, as McCormick actually prided himself upon his differences with the people of Baldric. He enjoyed his distinctiveness in the town that he had learned to love at an early age. In his earlier years, McCormick was a traveling salesman who traveled into, through, and quickly out of the town after a brief affair with the town trollop. Shortly thereafter, McCormick returned to Baldric to purchase a homestead and pursue his careers. He attempted to become a historian and a fledgling scientist. Unsuccessful at both, McCormick maintained a diminishing bank account. To mitigate his financial situation, the man entered into the business of invention. With six patents, and a seventh underway, he was still awaiting profitable leverage within the world of scientific innovation. First though, he pursued a differed aspiration which would be revealed soon enough to the twins.

McCormick bounded down the lane and unintentionally entertained the female who imitated the walk that the man displayed. Trixie began to tug on Einar, pulling him faster so that they could keep up with the man's pace. The girl's force of excitement of a new adventure brimmed through her smile and her step, even if deep down, her conscious still struggled with the day's events. McCormick was a nice diversion.

The home was discretely hidden away from the road, and the contents therein were even more so. McCormick enclosed the windows with the finest of timber stolen from the stockpiles around town. The man was thrifty and private; he did not necessarily abide by Baldric's economic code.

McCormick suddenly spoke, as if he and his visitors had been holding a conversation the entire time, the entire length of the driveway. "I knew your mother."

"Of course you did," Einar sarcastically retorted. He waited for his sarcasm to be understood and acknowledged.

McCormick nodded, rightfully so. This prompted Einar to continue. "Most male inhabitants of this town had been acquainted with our deceased mother. Why is this a topic of conversation? Why do you impede on our progress home?" Although Einar assumed that his mother was sexually deviant with all of the male members of the town, he did not recall McCormick listed in Lola's diary. Perhaps it was an oversight on the woman's part. And, although Einar knew that he and Trixie could turn around and leave, he was interested in McCormick's interest in them. Curiosity edged him forth.

Before answering Einar's questions, McCormick opened the door. Its hinges, covered in rust and obvious wear, crackled upon opening. Paint hung loosely off of the doorway. Einar and Trixie entered the dilapidated, dark portal into McCormick's life. The man had waited for this moment. The ground floor of the abode was nothing spectacular; it was a replica of much of the homes in Baldric. The first level, though, was not the intentional destination, McCormick's true, personal life was hidden away in the bottom floor of the structure. That was where he perfected his craft. McCormick spoke again, still avoiding Einar's question. "Follow me."

As he led the twins through the maze of piled boxes and books, McCormick was unaware as to how he was going to introduce his passions, himself, and his personal agenda to the twins. The man led his followers into his subterranean crypt. The faux medals of his ensemble clinked against the bronzed buttons of his heavy wool coat with each dooming step down the wooden stairs.

At the bottom of the staircase, the man finally responded to Einar. "Your mother and I shared a very special bond," he answered. McCormick's cordial eyes and peculiar resemblance to the twins calmed any distress they may have had after following the man into his basement. Both Einar and Trixie were innocently unaware of the dangers in the world. But, McCormick was harmless. As his feet settled upon the cold, cement floor, McCormick reached up and tugged on the string hanging from the wooden ceiling. With one pull, florescence flooded the basement and flaunted the littered laboratory. Einar and Trixie remained standing on the descending wooden floorboards. Both twins inspected the area filled with beakers and flasks, piles of metals, and bottles of solvents and liquids. The man became more apparent to the twins. His suiting showed soiled wear, and the brazen attributes scraped of any particular newness. McCormick's stint as an alchemist was successful to a minor extent, as denoted by his buttons.

"Apparently, many people could claim the same." Einar figured that McCormick's "special bond" was a euphemism for something more devious. In defense of McCormick, he was literally and figuratively correct. Einar was increasingly frustrated with the man who was being so vague. "How are you, specifically, affiliated with Lola? Why are you associating with my sister and I?" he asked. After posing his questions, Einar looked around the man's makeshift lab and interrupted the silence, as clearly, McCormick was not prepared to answer the former two questions. "What is all of this?" he questioned. He figured that Trixie wanted to know the same thing. She did.

McCormick held out his hand, showcasing the outcome of his brilliance. "These," he responded, "are my experiments."

Einar was leery. "What types of experiments?"

"That is not my part of my agenda today." It wasn't. He continued, "But someday, I will show you." And, someday, that was going to be his intention.

"So, you have an agenda?" Einar asserted.

"Yes, I have welcomed you into my home…to meet you,"

McCormick responded.

"Meet us? Why?"

Einar was starting to have doubts about his and Trixie's decision to follow the man. He turned to look at the top of the stairs and grazed Trixie's arm to alert her that he was ready to exit. McCormick witnessed this subtle movement, and consequently decided to be clearer about his intentions. Yes, he clearly had an objective, but unlike many of the people who wanted to take advantage of Einar and Trixie, McCormick's intent was in the best interest of the twins.

"Lola and I are rightful birth parents."

This statement confused Trixie who assumed that she had other siblings, perhaps ones who were not as demanding and pushy as Einar. Amazingly, she knew what a birth parent was, in part because Lola had always reminded Einar, "I am your birth mother. You do as I say."

Einar, on the other hand was not nearly as confused as his counterpart. "Rightful birth parents to whom?" he asked the man. Einar already assumed he knew the answer.

"Einar," McCormick looked at the male twin, his son, and then he turned to look at Trixie, his daughter, "Einar, Trixie, you are my children." McCormick regretted the use of the word "children". Einar and Trixie were visibly adults. They were adults who resembled him with their freckled faces and jutting ears.

"We, Mr. McCormick, are not children, obviously!" Einar caught the faulted man and was not going to allow the man to demean him and his sister, although that was not at all what McCormick intended.

"Yes, I understand this. What I am trying to say is that I am your father." And then he explained. Shortly after McCormick returned to Baldric, eight and a half months after he had quickly exited, he heard the scandalous gossip running through town. He went to visit Lola shortly after she gave birth. She shunned him, knowing that she did not want a male attachment; children were enough baggage. Her life had changed enough after meeting the man, and, as she said, "You need to be kind enough to leave me, us, alone." McCormick was kind, so he fathered from afar, far away from Lola's sights. Although McCormick never had any face-to-face interaction with his offspring, he did spend many afternoons and evenings fending off the curious, meddling people who attempted, for thirty years, to see the twins close up. He guarded the Smith household carefully when Lola was not around.

This information was stunning to the twins, and Einar, for a brief moment, was unsure how to respond. He did though. "What do you want with us?" he asked.

"I want to help you," the father responded.

Einar's response was forceful, "Much to your chagrin, we do not covet nor do we desire your assistance."

"Understood. I just think it was time to divulge the truth. You do not have to accept anything from me. I do not want to harm you." The latter of McCormick's statement could have been suggested earlier. It may have kept Einar from being so tense; thus his reaction may have been a bit more pleasant.

"We must leave. We have a career to which we need to attend in the morning." Einar poked Trixie who was still staring at the man, her father. She was dumb and dumbfounded (more of the latter).

"Here," McCormick reached into the interior pocket of his and pulled out two pictures. "Take these," he requested.

Trixie held out her hand and took the photos from the man. Trixie liked pictures, which is exactly what she said when she accepted the gifts. "Ooohhh! I like pictures."

"Keep these, to, at least, remind you of this day."

"Okay," the girl responded.

Neither Einar nor Trixie spoke as they walked up the stairs in the house of the man who was their father. Before leaving the house and entering the darkness of the outside, Trixie glanced at the photos that showed McCormick at the forefront and her and her brother in the background, pretending to be fencing experts. Trixie remembered many moments like that growing up. Her memories did not include McCormick watching from afar. She liked the pictures anyway.

"So, I have a father?" Trixie asked as she slowly walked home with her brother.

Einar was contemplative for a moment, but soon responded. "Yes, Trix, you and I have a father."

SIXTEEN

And the Earthen Ground will Shake

It only took twenty-four hours for Tolbett's Hill to be majestically decorated and the workers aptly prepared for what was the biggest annual event in Baldric. It only took twenty-four hours for Einar to adore the place, and it only took Trixie twenty-four hours to abhor the place. These feelings did not alleviate when the twins went home and then, the following day, when they returned. The news of the identity of their father was far from Einar's thoughts; he was anxious to be a part of Kluge's masterpiece.

The twins' arrival to the carnival grounds was a breathless task; the jaunt up the hill was trying, especially for Einar and Trixie, or their aliases Ein and Ix. When they did arrived at the foot of their tent, Trixie was apprehensive about entering. She clenched her photos, the ones given to her by McCormick, which were also the ones that she slept with underneath her pillow. And, she stood caressing the photos.

"What is your motive?" Einar asked. "We, as Einix, must enter."

"I..." Trixie knew that she had to come up with some sort of excuse, or otherwise, her brother would push her forward. "I want to wait."

"For what are you lingering?"

Trixie was confused by the use of the word lingering, but the sight of Kluge, like it usually did, distracted her thoughts. "Kluge!" she yelped. Kluge always calmed the girl's distress.

The proximity of the gap between Kluge and the EINIX tent was diminishing until Kluge was standing next to Einar and Trixie. He eyed the twins but said nothing. Without even gesturing the twins, Kluge sauntered into EINIX. They followed and waited for further instruction. As he would soon unveil to the twins, he was there to ensure that the performers were properly prepared for the onslaught of visitors who were willing to pay to see them.

"Are you ready?" Kluge asked as he attempted to excite the duo.

Einar was unsure as to how to answer the question, so he questioned the inquisition. "For what did we have to prepare?"

Kluge's initial question was meant to enhance the twins' excitement and anticipation of being a part of such a spectacular moment. Anyone who was employed by the Kluge family usually was.

Kluge didn't feel like conversing or maintaining any cordiality with the twins any further, so he summoned and then shoved Einix into the box that only maintained room for breathing and few movements. He then quickly shut the door that was drilled with a multiplicity of holes to allow air to infiltrate the container. "I will return later. Until then, the more money you make for the circus, the more money you earn. We all like money." Kluge advancing them into the container was the last human contact that the twins would have for hours. He quickly latched and locked the confinement and escaped the tent. The twins' eyes settled upon the colorful cloth that domed over the plastic.

Within moments, Ix, the name bestowed upon Trixie by the circus, distorted her body to find more room for the breadth of her being. To no avail, she was more confined than she had ever been with Ein, the name bestowed upon Einar by the circus.

Ein let the girl's awkward movements, no matter how invasive to his own body, to overtake the small space until he could, with his masculine stature, slowly nudge her closer to the wall. Ix finally found a space. Her head rested upon the strong, stable wall. It was neither roomy nor comfortable for either of the twins.

The curtain soon unveiled the first of many spectators.

"Oh children, look at you! Do you dance? Dance for me!" Aunt Evelyn was entirely too enthusiastic as she asked the twins to dance. The aunt skipped around and held a cup of beer that sopped over the lip with every movement. She flailed her arms and spun around, and around, and around. Before Aunt Evelyn could even witness the scene, the obscenity by nature inside of the box, the drape closed. It opened once she fitted another coin into the slot. This time, she paid more attention to the box instead of performing a one man tango. She screamed her wishes repeatedly and eyed the structure with utmost attention.

Only being able to see, not clearly hear the spectators, the twins were unaware as to what Aunt Evelyn was slurring until she realized the barrier between her and the twins. Communication was nearly improbable. She approached the structure and laid her mouth ever so slightly onto the smooth surface. "Dance, dance, dance!" Cautiously articulating the words, the woman finally conveyed her wishes as clearly as she could have.

In an attempt to follow the aunt's instructions while anticipating earning more coins from her, Ein collided with Ix to forge an impromptu dance, just like Trixie had done the day before. While peering at the face of the aunt that was at times distraught and at times amused, Ein lost sight of the innocent movement he was trying to coerce Ix into displaying. The swathe again blocked the image of the twins just in time for Ein to gather his entrepreneurial senses before his utter, painful boredom took over. The rapid movement of the fine piece of cloth continued until Aunt Evelyn also became bored with the sight that she was actually more accustomed to seeing than most everyone else in the town. It was the cage that allured her and then inhibited her amusement as the twins, mainly the male, joggled, about.

The curtain continued its fluid motion, following the track, back and forth, back and forth. At times, it sealed the sights of the bright lights streaming in from the outside world, and then it opened to exhibit the liveliness and excitement of the circus. Of course, the twins could not actively partake in the events. Ein, though, was inspired by more of a force than the bright lights and gloriously muted sounds. He was inspired by the sounds that came from the clank of metal hitting metal.

Throughout the evening and into the depths of the night, the mechanical obstruction unveiled a myriad of patrons standing in the tent of EINIX. With every new shiny coin entered into the slot, Ein did his best to encourage and crash and collide into the other idle twin. He hoped that she would dance or at least move or sway from side to side.

Instead, Ix opted to stare. For some time, she impersonated a mannequin staring back at the ogling faces. When doing so, Ix witnessed the devastating, malevolent reactions of the spectators. These included the laughs, the giggles, the looks of sheer awe, and the glares of disgust. She liked the man who claimed to be her father because he did not, in the short time that she knew him, look at her that way. But, he was not there to rescue her.

After a few hours, Baldric's Bapterian reverend, a man held in high regard, made his way into the tent to view the portable shelter and its contents that were far from angelic. Bearing an aluminum cross that was decorated with the most brilliant of fake gems, the religious man disbursed ample coinage into the collection box. As the cloth unveiled the scene, he waved the holy necklace in front of the twins and attempted to hypnotize them of their individual beliefs. Then, the reverend reached into his jacket and grasped a bottle of holy water. He began to sprinkle it around the structure. His countenance showed no emotion, and he mouthed no words for the twins. This left them befuddled and confused, although the demonic aversion was nothing but simple entertainment for the male twin, even if he was the one contained and expected to be the spectacle.

In an inappropriate attempt to lure Ix into a conversation, Ein wondered aloud, "If we were deceased, would this be how people view us?"

"Like Lola?" she asked. As unlikely as it was, Ix was trying to find her own identity, one that could separate her from the only memories that she had of family. She was finally becoming aware of who she was and who she wanted to become.

"Yes, Trix, like Lola." Ein continued, "Would they make peculiar faces?" Ein knew that Ix liked to make those faces. He thought the mere mention of it would enliven her.

"Like me?" she asked.

"Yes, Trix, faces like you made."

Ix was thoughtful for a moment. During the entire conversation, it distracted her enough to not pay attention to the people.

Just with this minute thought, Ein too became quite distracted about this idea. He envisioned Lola lying in the casket, a mental memento he held onto so tightly. He imagined her swimming in the fires of Hell. This sole thought made him slightly content, amoral, but content. And oddly, Ein realized that the situation, in which they found themselves, was comparable to calling hours for the dead, except this was a wake for the alive and healthy Ein and Ix. People danced, people shrieked, people stared, people cried…yes, it was a wake, and it was quite ironic.

When the twins had no further inclination to further the conversation, the brief moment of solitude was interrupted by Madam Bovine. She walked into the tent, sashayed up to the coin receptacle and dropped the quarter into the slot. When the curtain opened Madam Bovine, just like Aunt Evelyn, closely placed her lips upon the outside surface. She had a message.

Once her lips were close enough to the structure so that Ein and Ix could understand, she mouthed the words, "Hue will see big changes." She raised her crystal ball to the twins who stared into the clear, circular object. Inhaling a large breath, as if to blow her ancient wisdom into the sacrificial cage, she repeated the phrase again by exhaling her vision onto the hard surface. Her clairvoyance was perhaps a day late.

Just as the Madam dispelled the fortune, the curtain closed. And, the twins did witness big changes. The movement of the curtain soon unveiled a new sight. What they saw was quite a change from the sight of the wrinkled woman with a turban on her head. The patron was the more beauteous, young Ms. Jefferson.

Melanie Jefferson, in hopes to see the twins through a commoner's lens, entered the tent. With their confinement, the twins could not startle the girl who was quite frightened at the theater earlier that week. Ms. Jefferson, just like many of the other perverse folk, pretended to lift her shirt and wanted the twins to do the same. She wanted them to show themselves and show what was underneath that baggy sheath that they called clothing.

The night continued with the same scene over and over for the twins. Several of the children and some of the adults who entered felt the need to pound on the structure or wipe their dirty, popcorn oiled hands down the structure. When the latter occurred, it created a nasty glaze that barred the twins from seeing out clearly. These Neanderthal motions happened even with the sign that aptly read, "This box is filled with electric currents. Do not touch." The sign did not deter any of the imbeciles. Anyhow, it was clearly a lie, as nobody, even if they did touch the structure, had been electrocuted or even shocked, much to Ix's dismay.

With all of the incessant fondling of the box, Ix became relieved when the curtain closed, and the hands and other nasty body parts that slivered down the outside of the plastic disappeared from Ix's sight. Ultimately, the distressed female became notably more content every time the curtain closed. Ein, the amateur entrepreneur, became notably distraught each time the curtain closed.

As much as the situation should have melded the twins even closer, it separated them emotionally. Ix rested her head upon the hard surface of the wall that surrounded her and began to weep uncontrollably. She slathered her moist sweat-ridden hands against the wall and then crumpled them into fists as they lost strength and moved downward. The remnants of dirt streaked down the inside of the structure. As her hands gave in to emotional distraught, her tears did too as they tarnished her innocent face and dripped onto the surface. They then squeezed past her rosy cheek and streamed down the entire length of the acrylic. The images reminded her of the day earlier when her own ingenuous moment was spoiled. Never had she been so confined and so raped of her individuality.

Ein was encouraged by everything that abhorred Ix. He admired the spectators and played the role that he thought was fit for him and his sister. She gawked at the people staring at her. He had his sight on a goal. She had her sight on freedom. Yet, nobody was going to stop Ein, especially not his sister who just wouldn't understand, and everybody was going to ignore the reactions coming from the naïve girl.

Ix never moved from that position, regardless of the force of Ein's arm that attempted to entice any movement at all from his sibling. She continued weeping.

The shade that shielded the twins from the external world remained closed for some time, and Ix's anxiousness to be released overcame her senses. She started banging rapaciously on the plastic cage. Soon, the screaming followed. "Let me out! Please, let me out!" she demanded. The girl's hysteria continued for several minutes, and the shadow of the cover seemed to darken the chamber with her every breath that was spent to alert any mortal creature of her dire situation.

"Shhh… they will liberate us soon," Ein tried to explain. Yet, Ein's hushes and sweet pats on her shoulder, nearly the only part of her body that he could reach, did no good for the female twin who continued her rants and uncontrollable sobbing that interrupted Ein's articulate demands.

Soon enough though, the image of Einix appeared to another curious patron. The latter of the Einix found strength to halt her frenzy. The salty liquid stopped its cascade and just swarmed in her eyes. The tears awaited the next fit of emotion.

As the patron stepped forth, the small man's peculiarities and defiant height became apparent, and Ix realized that it was Morton. He was garbed in the most peculiar of costumes; he had been dismissed from his trade for the evening. In hopes to spend some appropriately qualifying time enjoying the circus, Morton weaved in and out of the tents, just to see what it was all about. Plus, he was quite quizzical about the twins and their duty of expertise which seemed much more interesting than his as a clown. He found contact with children and menacing adults to be wholly repulsive, but he did find a way to have solace throughout the evening by mimicking the twins' Aunt Evelyn's flask-carrying abilities. Morton hid the black market flagon in the belt of his oversized pants and proudly showed the twins as soon as the curtain opened.

The drunken intoxication allowed brief comic relief to Ix, who chuckled from the sight of the miniscule clown outfitted in the most colorful and bushy wig that was almost too large for his small head. His face was overwhelmed by the red foam circular nose. Just as Ix found innocuous reprieve, the image of the jester veiled, and the twin was again drowning in her own personal swamp of betrayal. Morton, though, was sure to spend plenty of his quarters that he randomly earned, or stole, on the twins.

With repetitious openings of the moving cloth, Ix was repeatedly amused by the midget and then repeatedly devastated by the disappearing figure. It became incidentally emotional for the girl until Morton ran out of quarters, and Ix's madness fully took over.

Thrashing Ein against his side of the box, Ix used all of her force to take out her sheltered sensations on the Ein who was visibly content with the job that they were instructed to follow. After moments of more scenic-less displays, Ix hoped the clown would return once more. When all was naught, she slid down the side of the container and pulled Ein with her. She settled at the bottom of the structure to continue her sobbing while Ein huddled over her.

A vast span of two minutes elapsed until movement once again interrupted the emotional display. The curtain opened one final time for the evening, and again, Ix's emotions halted. Ix hoped the visitor would once again be the short little clown who always provided ample entertainment for the twin who was expected to do the same. Ein used his muscular force to pull Ix up and hold her in an upright direction. But, she stumbled once again after realizing that the patron was not her friend. The image was less clear and much taller.

Just as the figure was about to clarify itself, it moved away from the opening. Its identity was only partially revealed when an appendage of the unknown snuck between the split in the cloth. The hand of its invisible master caressed a crisp fifty-dollar bill against the human sized canister. The other arm, belonging to the same unknown master, plastered itself and another bill against the machine. Both parts of Einix could slightly hear a bellied laughter coming from beyond the bills and beyond the arms. It was, of course, the giddy laughter from Kluge who was there to dismiss the twins for the evening. As soon as the sound of delight was heard, there was no need for the figure, which jiggled the coin box and listened intently to the coins splash from wall to wall of the metal container, to reveal itself physically.

Pleased with the amount of coinage left in the container, Kluge made his way to the hindquarters of the structure. The unlocking of the mechanism seemed to take forever, but as soon as Ix felt the rush of a fresh breeze scented with buttery popcorn and animal feces, she let out a huge breath, as if holding the stale air for the entirety of the ordeal, because that was what the night became, an ordeal.

Ix quickly stepped out of the box and pulled Ein a bit more than he expected. As Trixie was planted firmly on the brown, arid soil, her counterpart was soon fumbling out of the box. Einar fell to the ground, atop the hay. His eyes darted to the money that lured him upright.

"Fabulous! You guys were perfect. Just perfect!" Kluge exclaimed. He could not contain in his appreciation for the twins. "If you can keep it up, you will be earning much more than this. Much more." Kluge handed each of the twins the bills, based on their earnings, and this time, it was much more than Einar expected. Trixie found little solace in the exchange. She did not actually know how to use the monetary unit; she was, after all, a female in the town of Baldric where economic status was determined by promiscuity.

It had only been one day and several hours, and the twins had become, at least in Einar's eyes, successful. Einar turned to Trixie. "Yes," he said, "this is economically advantageous for us. What Gertrude Sconch had determined was correct; we will be stars!"

Kluge was impressed with the enthusiasm, and as he exited, he attempted to encourage the twins even more. "Find a way to become more appealing, more entertaining. Be the savior of the circus, one that will make me more money. More money."

Einar knew what a savior was, and Kluge's remarks made him intensely intrigued with Kluge. He filled the shoes of a role model that Einar never thought would exist. It was a prideful moment for Einar. He was a savior. Trixie, on the other hand, thought nothing of Kluge's exiting remarks. She just continued staring at the bill that she could not even fathom using. For one brief moment, losing her identity was just a minor figment of her imagination, as the fifty consumed most of her attention but still did little to calm her distress.

SEVENTEEN

A Substance of Intrigue will Bake

The twins were released from their role as the EINIX. They exited the tent and stepped onto the dirt path that was scattered with litter. It was a sight that proved what an underdeveloped society Baldric had become. The trash receptacles were strategically placed one hundred feet apart, so there was no excuse for the pile of trash atop the dirt covered dump.

Aside from witnessing the aftereffects of a grotesque display of laziness, the twins also witnessed Morton eagerly racing toward them. He was attentive to gossip about the celebration of the opening night at the circus. "The Opening Night Soiree", as it was so appropriately named, was the gathering of all of the infamous circus workers; it was an inauguration of another splendid season of circustry.

Knowing all about the event, Morton insisted, "We absolutely have to attend this party."

Einar and Trixie, stretching their aching muscles because of their confinement, sat atop the dirt mound and peered down at the midget. "They have games," he coerced.

Trixie, taking a strong liking for games, questioned the remark. "Games? What kind of games?"

"Oh you know." Morton, failing in his attempt to think of an assortment of lovely games that Trixie would be aware of, began to skip nearer the local tavern, the location of the fête, which honored all of the uniqueness the circus had to offer. Silently,

Morton compelled the twins to follow the tune of his magical, inaudible flute.

The urging worked, and the twins followed Morton. Their five minute conversation during their five minute walk was consumed by the previous night's events. Morton listened intently and secretly wished that he too could have met the father of the twins. But, he was gracious for the time apart from them. It was sexually advantageous for him, although monetarily detrimental. Morton needed to increase his understanding of the town's monetary intricacies.

The conversation, without one mention of Morton's crazy night, ceased when the twins were standing in the center of the pub, a shanty, undersized enclosure that often entertained the likes of few. The dark wooden floors and walls lent themselves to a history of drinkers. The beams rose high into the ceiling. The thick smoke of cigarettes and cigars ascended just as high to meet the beams and cover them until the smoke dissipated to impenetrable, blackish soot. The twins and Morton were overwhelmed by the organized chaos.

"Whoa,"Trixie remarked. She had never seen a place like this.

The assemblage of circus folk and a few brave townspeople filled the bar. The mass crowd caused the Russian contortionists to push and shove a multitude of people to clear a makeshift dance floor, in the middle of which the twins stood. They watched the man and woman limber around and on top of one another while twirling and pivoting to every beat of the jukebox music that resounded through the hostelry that doubled as an inn for those who were fated with insufferable, blacking out intoxication. They were circus folk after all.

"Vat do you do?" The lithe female, hanging upside down in a dancer's dip, asked the twins who were unable to mosey through the crowd with ease or even at all.

"We..." Einar could not necessarily define what they did

because it was seemingly nothing. He couldn't tell that to the working elastic Russians, namely Ivanna and Ivan.

Anyway, before Einar could answer, even if he wanted to, Trixie interjected, "That's pretty." She was referring to the woman's glittering ensemble that held snugly onto the woman's bodice. The clothing was bright, bruise purple, and it shimmered in the pelting light from the hanging disco ball.

Ivanna thought Trixie referred to the golden chalice filled with vodka that the woman was swinging around. She raised her glass to the girl, "Vant some?" she inquired.

The sweat and the tears of earlier inflicted a ravenous thirst in Trixie. She accepted the goblet and took a swig. Her face immediately puckered up as she handed the drink back to the female. The puckering and the contact made her feel like an individual human again, and she liked that.

Einar noticed nothing of the exchange, as the male, Ivan, less drunk than his counterpart, held onto the wavering Ivanna and questioned the twin. "How you two move?"

Einar thought it was an interesting question considering the male's elasticity, which he showed with every move and lift of his female. He didn't answer the man. Tired of the casual conversation, Einar tugged on Trixie's arm in an effort to prompt her to go, but she was too busy infusing the liquid offerings that the Russian female continued to share.

"Valk for me," Ivan demanded.

By this time, the contortionist's street stock was lowering because of the twins, who everybody cautiously eyed. The twins were a spectacle, even without doing anything.

Not noticing the stares, Einar and Trixie spent most of the time exchanging looks between each other and the Russians; the effects of the vodka blurred Trixie's vision as she waved her hand erratically in front of Einar's face and tried to earn his attention while simultaneously clarifying the image that she saw. Although nearing inebriation, Trixie, finally acknowledged the demand made earlier by the male contortionist; his voice registered many seconds after he spoke. After the delay, Trixie imitated the most cautious of tightrope walkers. She turned gracefully and pulled her brother with her while she staggered and waltzed through the small bit of space allotted for the twins. She did her best to avoid any of the barstools or people; this included avoiding the midgets who jutted out from their rightful places; most were situated at the bar. All of Trixie's steps were purposeful. The twins moved from one spot to another, as if the entire world was watching; this was one of the few times Trixie would have gladly accepted others to see her. She then held out her arm for another sip of the magical beverage.

Einar pulled Trixie away from the frenzy, although he never once questioned the liquid inside of the cup from which the girl took another sip. As Einar's tug furthered them from the crowd, the contortionists, enamored by the twins, trailed them. Morton finished perusing the joint and joined the twins with two brimming cups of red punch. "Want some?"

Everyone was at his or her most generous in times of intoxication.

"What is it?" Einar asked before he sipped the concoction.

The midget just shrugged his shoulders but added, "They said something about a punch from Peter's, whoever that might be."

Einar took the cup and then took a swig, at which point he spat it out onto the midget's face. "This has liquor in it!" He knew because he could nearly taste the liquor on his dear aunt's breath every time she spoke. It tasted like it smelled, and the drink surprised Einar. He loosened his grip which was keeping Trixie, who was swaying from side to side, upright. The girl tilted sideways toward the concrete floor.

The contortionists, costumed in cardboard top hats and feather boas, approached and tempted the twins to twirl and coil, movements of which the Russians were quite fond. Einar preferred to move forward into the more vacant area of the corner. The colorful entourage followed but something soon diverted their attention.

When the twins and Morton approached the corner table, a man, dressed in the finest of fatigues, rose. He immediately recognized the twins, and Einar did the same of him. McCormick spoke, "Share this seat with me." The previous day's meeting weighed heavily on McCormick's mind. He wanted to help the twins, even if they didn't realize that they needed help. So, he followed the twins around, in what would have been a creepy stalkerish kind of way if he wasn't their father.

Without delay, Einar situated Trixie into the round, wooden booth. A day later and many dollars wealthier, Einar did not feel the need to be harsh. He was content, honestly content. He proceeded to slide closer to his twin to make room for the midget.

When the twins and Morton finally settled around the round table, Morton interjected the awkward silence between the twins and the weird man. "Who is that?" He pointed to McCormick and bobbed his head in the direction of the man.

Einar looked at McCormick for approval. McCormick nodded his head before Einar commented, "Morton, this is our father, Mr. McCormick."

Morton was not finished with his inquiry. "And how did you prove that you are the father of these fine specimen?" Morton was leery of the odd man's intentions.

McCormick did not flinch; he did not waver. He answered as honestly as he could. "When I was in the military, before ever meeting Lola Smith, I was in a drug screening program. I was introduced to many hazardous medications, many of which, in retrospect, were attributed to birth defects. I enjoyed an encounter with Lola, and after the appropriate gestation period, Einar and Trixie were born. When I found out about the birth of the twins, I was certain that they were my offspring. It was their birth defect that alerted me to this fact."

Einar quickly responded, "We do not have a birth defect. We are just like everyone else."

"You are similar to everyone else. You do have individual personalities and different aspirations, but you are, pardon my terminology, defected."

"Then," Einar prompted, "what is our ailment?"

McCormick avoided the question. "I have been experimenting."

"Yes, the experiments. What types of experiments?" Einar questioned, after remembering mention of them the day prior. Einar was interested in the man of science. He was much less interested in the man as his father. McCormick was okay with that.

"I have been practicing experiments to cure you." And, he had been practicing.

"So, you do suggest that we have a specific ailment, a specific defect?" Einar asked in response.

"It is specific. It is rare."

Einar knew that he and Trixie were different. Trixie, although not cognizant of it at that moment, knew that she and Einar were different. They were rare.

Not wanting to delay the diagnosis any longer, McCormick revealed the secret. He had waited thirty years. "You are conjoined. You are separate individuals merged into one body. I have a cure." McCormick spent a large portion of his life as a self-proclaimed chemist. After months of toil, he transformed himself into Baldric's finest, yet only, pharmaceutical engineer. Baldric folk suffered from a multitude of illnesses, in part, because of their less than sanitary living conditions. McCormick, after meeting the twins, had set his sights on a much more momentous, although risky, cure.

Neither Einar nor Trixie fully understood their scientific diagnosis, as nobody ever took the time to explain their medical mystery until now. Within moments, Einar was accepting of the analysis. He looked at his body, their body. It had a name. And, it was the first time that somebody directly acknowledged their shared body. All that McCormick had hoped for was coming to fruition. He was single-handedly responsible for the bonded carcass, so he wanted to be responsible for separating them. He had studied his craft intently and waited for this day.

"I can cure you," he spoke. "You will live as individuals. When people see you, they will be in sheer awe of you. It won't be like the awe that you witness now. It will be astonishment that somebody, me, was able to give each of you your own lives. It will make us famous. I need this; you need this." McCormick was speaking directly to Einar. He knew that the male was the ultimate decision maker. And, he was correct. Einar's and Trixie's current situation would kill them sooner than later. Einar deserved to live life for himself. Trixie deserved to live life for herself.

Missing the entirety of the conversation, Trixie turned to Einar after hearing many voices but not listening to any of them. "Huh?" she questioned.

Einar explained the situation that was presented to him and Trixie. When describing the scenario, Einar every so often turned to McCormick to ensure that he was fully explaining the situation correctly. McCormick just nodded in agreement to Einar's explanation. Ultimately, the twins were going to help McCormick, and McCormick was going to help the twins.

Without further ado, without need for further explanation, McCormick slid off of the bench and waved Einar and Trixie toward the door. Morton pursued the twins outside until Einar turned and waved him away. This needed to be a moment between him and his sister...and their father.

McCormick was the savior for the evening for the twins, much like the twins were for Kluge. He led them to a back alley, toward his brown pickup truck where his experiment would be less visible. Wanting Einar and Trixie to be relaxed about their decision, the man reached into his olive fatigues and pulled out a stack of fives. "This is my life savings. It is insurance that your existence will be your own."

Einar reached for the money and almost did not realize how adamant he was against respecting McCormick the day prior. The man's expertise and the stack of cash made Einar respect and trust the man.

Trixie stood beside the pickup truck and wavered to and fro. Her fingers grasped the bed of the pickup held her off the ground. Einar felt the force of the girl brush up against his side; her head plopped upon his shoulder as her hand grasped the bed.

"How do we return the favor?"

"Your acknowledgment of our familial relationship and my genius are enough. Plus, this could make us all quite wealthy."

The thought of becoming rich with money was just a minute faction in Einar's plan to become a real, unjudged member of society. He was living a dream that few in the town of Baldric had the chance to live. He was earning a multitude of wages. It was more than he could have ever asked for, even if the money was distorting his reality while shaping his American dream. Plus, he dreamed of how much money he could actually earn on his own free will, yet still care for his sister who would also be free. Unfortunately, Trixie would be limited by the limitations of her knowledge and sense.

Einar's agreement was thoughtless at best. If he and Trixie were separated, they would not be stared at, they would not be the subject of gossip, and they would certainly not earn cash for work. It was ironic. They would become like everyone else in the town. This time, Einar was naïve. The situations offered to them were unique. Nobody earned cash, nobody, that was, except for Einar and Trixie together as one (and that one prostitute that Morton lent his wallet and himself to).

McCormick led the twins to the back of the pickup. "Lay here," he instructed as he pointed to the tarp that outlined the bed of his truck. The scientist then unleashed the homemade agent from the metal box situated next to Trixie. The man outfitted his appendages with metal sheaths that covered his hands and a welder's mask that he fit over his head while Einar laid and clenched the money he was about to earn. Trixie just looked at the box and then at the stars; the shiny stars glittered in the night's abyss. It was the last thing she would remember from that night.

McCormick prepped the twins' body with a numbing agent. He then took a solvent, his "separating mixture with a highly concentrated acid base". He held it above the fused, naked body. In one brief motion, he poured the mixture across the skin and muscle that bound the twins. The acid that hit the skin caused incessant burning and smoke. McCormick tossed the empty glass bottle to the side and picked up the other liquid he intended to discharge over the burns. As the acid ate away at the skin, the scientist then poured the soothing liquid onto the wounds. The acid continued spreading across the body and seeped only slightly below the deep tissue skin level. Anxious about this endeavor, McCormick began the process a bit too hastily, since the liquid interrupted the first solvent from motioning through the body. McCormick was clearly an amateur, an amateur with appropriate intentions.

When the beginning stages of the experiment were complete, McCormick hopped in the cab of the truck and sped away from the air that reeked of burnt epidermis. McCormick couldn't entirely escape the odor since the twins were still situated in the back. The calming breeze of the night air eased the pain as Einar attempted to sit up. He hoped to fully cure him and his sister of their ailment that he kept hidden deep within his conscious. He wanted to separate their being; two people could make much more money than one.

The crisp flesh just rustled from the movement. The acid mixture darkened their figures and then quickly dried up. It created a puddle of ash that fell to the floor of the bed and then fluttered out of the bed of truck when the cold air from the moving vehicle invaded the open space.

With nowhere to go, Einar just layed next to his sister and placed his head upon her shoulder. He fell soundly asleep while still grasping his compensation. In those moments before his slumber, Einar never once regretted the disfigurement, even if no one was cured.

EIGHTEEN

The Einix will Rise Again

For thirty years, neither twin accepted any proposal to be separated, literally. McCormick's elixir did not work as both men had planned, and ultimately, the girl was still attached to her brother. For nearly a lifetime, they shared one and a half livers, even after the experiment. Fate had different intentions. As Trixie slept, the alcohol she consumed infiltrated Einar's body. It slowly killed him. It was neither McCormick's success as a pharmaceutical genius and a caring father nor Einar's swift decision that allowed for the plan to come to fruition; it was the innocent entertaining of the female that finally destined the twins' removal from one another. If only the contortionists were not so alluring, perhaps sobriety would have been the result of the evening. Regardless, Trixie could not have wondered this in retrospect, as she had no clue as to her and Einar's whereabouts and their reasoning behind their whereabouts.

Throughout the night, the impact of the liquor, which pacified the female during the mutilation, became too overwhelming for Einar's half liver. While Trixie rested ever so soundly in the bed of McCormick's truck with the soothing liquor sweeping away her angst and pain, Einar did even more so as he slowly crept into an eternal slumber and joined his mother in an unknown place. He had reached what would have been the height of his career. It would have been all downhill from that night anyway. At least Trixie's life was salvaged, even if she was stuck in the medical hospital.

Amid the chaos of the emergency room, Trixie slept soundly and eventually awoke. Finally, she was fully devoid of any liquor in her system. On the hospital gurney with Einar next to her, Trixie's body rested upon the crisp, white sheets that rustled like the tarp where she laid to have the top layers of her skin eaten away. The room was scarce, except for a multitude of machinery she had never seen before, and the gadgets were much more complicated than what Mr. McCormick could have offered. Fortunately for the girl, McCormick's actions were quick once he thought that his experiment had turned deadly. He anonymously dropped the conjoined twins off at the emergency room entrance. He used the cash that he handed Einar to ensure that the twins would receive proper, prompt attention. He truly did not want to harm them. The past day's events frightened him, so he appropriately exited their lives. His seventh patent was certainly going to be denied.

Nobody except Einar was in the room when Trixie woke, so she did not worry about where or why she was there. She figured it was Einar's doing. She was obviously unaware of her actions. That was the beauty of being intoxicated. Trixie looked over at her peaceful brother and turned to fall asleep once again. The medication inundated her.

When she awoke the second time, Trixie was beneath a bright light. A masked man who breathed heavily through the greenish cloth that covered his mouth looked over the girl. Trixie waved her hand above Einar's face, to see if he woke with the same sight. "Do you think he can see me?" she asked. She was nearly giddy and unaware from all of the inoculations.

"I don't think so," the man replied.

Trixie, in an attempt to distract her brother, scrunched her nose and crossed her eyes. She overlooked the silent male twin. Nothing could distract him, the him that was lifeless, still attached to her.

"You cannot wake him. He is dead." The doctor, unaware that Trixie did not know the status of her attached brother, felt the need to reiterate the harsh reality to the female.

"Dead?" she repeated.

"Yes, he was declared incapacitated soon after your arrival. Furthermore, we are going to extract his body for science. We will, after you are feeling better, need you to examine the body to ensure it is Einar's, once it is removed."

Trixie sat up as far as she could with the weight of her dead brother holding her back from hitting her head on the overhead light. "Science? Removed?" Trixie was caught up in the verbal rhetoric. It took her a moment to understand that the doctor was having a conversation with her, not Einar, her. After the doctor nodded in response to her questioning, Trixie soon realized the severity of the moment, " How will I,"Trixie was unsure of how to end the question. She couldn't finish, so she just tilted back onto the bed.

"No worries. You will be just fine, as soon as we remove him from your body." The doctor's voice was calming, and Trixie did not have any more worries, in part from the fabulous anesthetics that soon erased her memory and senses just long enough for her to lay on the operating table and have her brother surgically removed from her forever.

When she awoke from her slumber a third time, Trixie was in recovery, and a myriad of folk, including Morton, Kluge, and Evelyn, peeped over her bed. The midget offered his support while the aunt just drank her calming concoction, and Kluge looked upon the new singleton with an odd excitement.

"Hi!" Trixie was happy to recognize the faces above her. She, realizing her own self, turned to her left to share the moment, but recognized, when looking at the vacant space next to her, that she had nothing to share. That was okay with her.

Beside her was only the crisp white sheet she remembered

from the day before; Einar was gone. She looked back up at the staring faces and back down at the unoccupied space. She then grasped her gown and opened it to look at the visible pink scars from the splashed acid; the scars were tattoos of the experiment gone askew. The ash was washed away when Einar's body was removed. Any other wounds, along with the repeated markings of slicing and stitches, were hidden away by white bandages and gauze that had remained wrapped around her body.

After days of uneventful healing, Trixie, still discombobulated, was eventually escorted into the hospital mortuary. The cold air raided her senses as she, shivering, cautiously leaned over the metal cold chamber, draped in clear, sterile plastic. "Is he dead?" Trixie asked the poignant question to the hospital orderly, although all she wanted to do was shake the body incessantly for any response.

"Yes," the orderly answered, as he waited for the emotion of grief to creep in and devastate the other half of the deceased twin. "This is your brother, correct?" The hospital, although already knowing the answer, needed formal confirmation to allow the postmortem events to fully take place.

"Yes," Trixie answered as she peered down at the toe tag, which was adequately marked "Einar Smith". The name startled her for a bit. She actually hoped to read Einix just for closure, but she knew, in all desperation, that she needed to rise above the label that was not put to rest that day. She peeked over the impersonal casket once again and made some monstrous faces at her brother. She was seemingly unaware of the grave situation that lay in front of her. He would not wake, though, to remind her that he could not see the faces.

Feeling the oddness of the situation, the orderly carefully pushed the fragile twin to the side and allowed the shiny silver door to suction the cold air that wafted around the dead body. As Trixie turned to exit, the release of Einar's soul from her body and her mind caused her to smirk behind her stone-faced countenance. She knew that she could deem herself a Repubocrate. She knew that Einar's counting lesson was unnecessary as currency was going to be useless. Most importantly, she knew that she could appropriately repay Kluge, and that sheer satisfaction created the feeling of freedom that even memories could not absolve.

LaVergne, TN USA
30 May 2010
184486LV00005B/2/P